Moments

Moments

Subhash Jaireth

PUNCHER & WATTMANN

First published in 2015.

Published by Puncher and Wattmann
PO Box 441
Glebe NSW 2037

http://www.puncherandwattmann.com
fiction@puncherandwattmann.com

National Library of Australia
Cataloguing-in-Publication entry:

Jaireth, Subhash

Moments

ISBN   9781922186737

I. Title.
A821.3

Cover design by Matthew Holt

Printed by McPherson's Printing Group

Sponsored by

This project has been assisted by the Australian Government through the Australia Council, its arts funding and advisory body.

for HJ, KJ and MJ

Contents

Preface

In this collection of eleven short stories I continue the narrative experiment, which I started in the book *To Silence*. The three monologues in *To Silence* were conceived and structured as fictional autobiographies of three historically real figures. All eleven stories in this collection are also about historically real figures. In telling these stories I have relied on published biographical information. However biographical facts have been intertwined with fictional elements imagined by me. The imagination imparts emotional fibre to the stories. I call these stories fictional biographies (stories told in third-person voice) and autobiographies (stories told in first-person voice). However they should not be read and used as biographies. The sources of biographical material accessed for these stories are mentioned in the references at the end of the book.

Bach (Pau) in Love

Martita my darling is the marvel of my world. Each day I find something wonderful in her: the way she walks, turns her head, raises or lowers her arm; the way she does her hair or puts colour on her lips; and the way she just sits with me. Her presence bestows light and hope, setting aglow the world around me; and the light, I am glad, seems to last forever.

"What new wonder will she bring today?" I think each day. I live in anticipation, and this keeps me excited.

The other day she asked me about Bach's Cello Suite No. 2 in D minor: "Was Bach in love?" Most probably he was, as I have been since the day I saw Martita walk into my life for the very first time with her cello. I owe everything in my life to the cello, good and bad, although the bad was most probably of my own making. In the cello I have found nothing but benevolence—even in the instrument that my dear father conjured many years ago. In the garden of a friend, he found a dry yellow gourd, long and narrow, and asked Peret, the old barber, to help him wind a solo string on it. The thrill I experienced that day was immense, and even today as I recall the moment, I am overcome by fear and excitement. I remember trying a few scales first, and then I played Schubert's 'Serenade'. I was nine, then—still unprepared to face Bach, but the gourd was perhaps the first premonition, or warning, I suppose, that I should be ready to welcome him. That happened after four years, and I know that this was the most appropriate moment: only a day before, my dearest father had given me the most wonderful birthday present—my first full-sized cello.

The Grützmacher edition of the cello suites, which we stumbled upon in an old beachside shop in Barcelona, has remained with me, and although I don't use it any more, its presence in the house is a blessing. For the past eighty years, I have started each day with Bach: I go to the piano, and play preludes and fugues. "It's a benediction on the house," my darling Martita doesn't fail to remind me, and she is right. But she should know that without her, even Bach would turn his back on me.

I like the house Martita has made for us. It sits high on the hills overlooking the city of San Juan. I miss the sea and the beach, although from the terrace I can still see the sea lining the horizon, and at nights when quiet falls I hear it whisper in the voice of my mother, "Don't worry Paulito; I won't abandon you," before dispatching wafts of cool breeze. I doze off in the chair, soothed by the noises Martita makes in the house, and in my sleep I wait for her to wake me with a kiss.

She knows that I miss my walks with her on the beach, but she is right that the noise from the airport has become unbearable. The city is growing, and if everyone wants to build a house close to the beach, let them do it. The sea is for everyone. "You are right, Paulito," Martita encourages me. I like the way she calls me Paulito, when no one is around, as if she isn't my young and beautiful wife, but my dear mother. "You are my mother, my daughter and my woman," I told her once. "When I make love to you, I make love to them all." I was afraid that my muddled thought might upset her, but it didn't, and I was pleased that she didn't reprimand me. "It's love, dear Paulito," she smiled.

I sometimes wonder if it is this love that has calmed me. I am very old now, and yet it seems all thoughts of death, I mean fear, have been cast away. It can knock at the door any moment, walk in and ask me to come and I'll leave without any hesitation, remorse or grief. Martita's love has brought contentment, relief and most of all peace.

The country house where we retreat for weekends is called El Pessebre, but Martita is the house where my heart has found the crib, the abode of peace. I say this so emphatically now because it wasn't always like that.

I nearly died ten years ago. Such a massive seizure, for a man who had lived eighty long years of joy and torment, could have been fatal. And yet I survived. Lying in the hospital then, I was scared of dying, because I didn't want to die; to live a few more years in the same house with Martita was my dream, and this dream kept me alive. Because I wanted to live so much, death standing at the door had come as a terrible fright. I must have prayed—I know I must have—and I am glad that I was spared. I was in love with Martita then as well, but that was a different kind of love: unsure, and that's why selfish, arrogant, unforgiving.

Martita nursed me in my illness and during the uncertain months of slow recovery. She walked with me every morning and diligently disciplined my craving for the cello, letting me play only for an hour or so on the piano. The cello was brought to me only for a few minutes just to let me hold the dear thing in my hand and feel that it was waiting for me to get better. I knew I had to be patient, hoping that my left hand and its fingers would regain the necessary strength. Hope is always tinged with fear, and the fear that my cursed hand would refuse to get better kept me awake at night. It was a strange feeling to find myself talking to my hand and fingers as if they weren't my own. I would remind myself often of the accident I had suffered climbing up Mount Tamalpais near San Francisco. Then, a boulder had mangled the fingers of that same left hand. Good, I had told myself then; I'll never have to play the cello again. It was silly, but what else could I have thought? All passion in the end enslaves you, and if I felt in bondage to Bach and music at that time, it was because I doubted my ability to make beautiful music each time I decided to play. A few months after the mishap, Gertrude Stein saw me in Paris with my left hand in a white plaster; she wasn't that famous then. "You look like El Greco's *Gentleman with His Hand on His Chest.*" I survived the ordeal of the accident on my own back then, but with my seizure ten years ago Martita helped me to pull through. And perhaps that's the reason I decided one day to ask her to marry me.

I am many years older than even her father, and to be honest I have often wondered what prompted her to say yes. She is so young for him, I am sure most people think, pitying her plight.

What most of us do in bed is I think a mere fraction of what might be called love; to make love is an odd expression: what precedes and what follows is I believe more profound. I wait anxiously for these moments, and they are truly of another, almost unworldly, order. Unworldly not because there is something mystical about them, but because of their profound mystery. Isn't it stupid or even arrogant of us to think that we can find a rational explanation for each and every thing in this world? Explanation, like unveiling, destroys the sanctity of the moment, the meaning of which we as yet don't know or will never know. The inability to know should never frustrate us, because who knows what knowing might bring us?

That's exactly what I told the young man who came to see me many years ago in Prades. I was walking back to the villa after my daily morning stroll. It was a warm autumn day. The light was bright, but not enough to hurt the eyes. I had turned to look back, to cast a quick glance in the direction of my friend, Mount Canigou — to salute, bow and acknowledge its presence — when I heard my ever-aware Follet bark and run through the front gate. I called her back; she stopped, turned her head towards me, the look asking me Are you sure?" in her doggy way. I was sure, because the young man sitting at the bottom of the steps looked sick and frightened. The long overcoat he wore had holes, the sole of his left shoe was broken and his eyes were intensely melancholic. A bag lay next to him on the steps, and beside it stood a violin in a case.

He got up on his feet and greeted me with a big smile that only lasted a few seconds. "I am sorry, *maître* Casals," he said, "to come unannounced and so early in the day."

"He is a German," I thought, listening to his heavy accent. I reprimanded myself for my inability to control a strong prejudice against the Germans who often came to see me.

"I must talk to you," he said, "about Bach and music." He looked at me, waiting for my reaction.

Must? I was surprised by the urgency of his tone. "I can't refuse him," I thought. "He needs help." I told him that I had to have a shower and something to eat, after which I would be ready to talk. He picked up his rucksack and violin and walked out through the gate, promising to return in an hour and a half.

He returned precisely an hour and a half later and found me sitting on the terrace. He walked up to me and waited to be invited to sit down.

We talked for a few hours. He played some Bach on his violin. Very ordinary, I have to say, but I was glad he knew that he wasn't a very good player. He came again the next day and the day after, and I came to know more about him. His name was Johann Sebastian Greitner. He didn't tell me his second name immediately, embarrassed perhaps that he shared it with Bach. When I think about him now, the thing that I found endearing in him was the feeling of embarrassment he displayed in whatever he said or did, as if his first impulse was not to draw attention to himself.

He was thirty, he said, and a communist. He had spent three years in a fascist prison near Leipzig, freed when the Red Army marched in. Before the war he had been a photographer who also liked to write about the photos he took. His mother, Anna, had been a violinist who had died giving birth to his younger sister. His father, Gottfried, had owned a little bookbinding shop and had been killed in the battles near Stalingrad.

Johann loved music, and because he didn't have much talent as a player he had learnt to listen and to think about music with empathy—not in terms of structure, style or composition, but as an entity that made the heart and body do the strangest things. He had received Bach from his mother as a sort of communion and had lived his whole life feeling blessed—even in the prison camp, where hunger and torture had ruined his health. The word communion he mentioned surprised me a little, because the daily tête-à-tête that I have with Bach is also a communion of a sort.

"What is so special about Bach?" I thought, doing my utmost to curb a smile, because I didn't want to hurt his feelings, or belittle his concern or his need to find an answer. It was quite clear that the question had a profound bearing on his life. He had invested (so it seemed) his whole heart and soul in it. It is one thing to be ready to encounter beauty, I wanted to tell him, but quite another to worry about its nature, power or reason. We feel blessed that it has come our way, bringing us joy, but we also feel lost and confused because we aren't sure if the moment will last or if it will come again. Both in joy and in sorrow lies the mystery of beauty.

Why is Bach so special? I too have asked this question. Each time I play something of his, my body turns itself inside out, baring its innermost being, and yet I have never been able to find an adequate explanation for why this might be. Why is this or that thing so beautiful, we ask ourselves, forgetting there are experiences that are hard to translate adequately into words. Words often fail, don't they? Perhaps that is why we humans must have felt the need to invent music. At first we turned the most ordinary of words into poems, hymns and songs, but as we began to sing them we realised that there were occasions when the words weren't so essential after all; that's when we decided, no, not to forget them completely, but just to push them into the background so that body and sound could reach perfect unison.

Listening to Johann that autumn, I felt that he was more desperate than I to find an answer. I was by then old enough to reconcile with the idea that it wasn't quite in our capacity to understand and explain every thing in this world.

Before the war, Johann told me, he had walked and cycled several times across the towns and cities where Bach had lived and worked. He showed me an old map of Thuringia, Saxony and Bohemia on which he had plotted the routes and places he had visited. Twice he had traced Bach's walk from Arnstadt to Lübeck so as to feel what a twenty-year-old Bach would have felt—thrilled, as we all know, by the hope of listening to Buxtehude on the organ.

There were hundreds of photos in Johann's rucksack, most of them black and white. He showed me some. "You don't like taking photos of people?" I asked him.

"That's right," he replied, embarrassed. His aim was to map the land: houses, rooftops, roads and tracks, rivers and bridges, trees and birds, churches and bell towers, hills and valleys, and horses, cows and pigs. He photographed people only if they were singing or playing an instrument.

He was, he explained, looking for clues.

He told me, "Beethoven named the slow movement of his Pastoral Symphony 'An der Bach' (by the brook). The name expresses the mood of the movement perfectly, but isn't it possible that Beethoven also wanted it to mean 'by the side of Bach'?"

Johann said these words and smiled. This made him appear young and happy, and before I could think of an answer for myself, he came up with the possible answer: "When I listen to Bach, I seem to turn into a fish."

"How wonderful," I thought because I have often felt the same. Playing Bach, I often think of water. It flows in and around me, and like a hollow reed I am cleansed of all my ills. The trouble is that such moments are always brief and invariably transient.

On the third day, Johann asked me to play the cello suites. Not the six as a whole, but only the preludes. I immediately understood his intention. I knew he wasn't lying when he said that he had heard my recordings of the suites. We spent a lot of time talking about the Suite No. 1 in G major and the Suite No. 2 in B minor. The contrast between the emotions they create is too stark: the first is joyful and optimistic; the second sombre, sad and melancholic. I was expecting that Johann would soon ask me if I knew the reason Bach had suddenly composed such delicate music, so precise in expression and so uniquely personal.

If I said "I don't know", it was because I sensed he had something to say and was keen for me to hear him out.

"Bach was in love," he said, and paused for a few moments. Realising that I wasn't going to interrupt, he told me the story he had conjured.

*

Bach was in love with Anna Magdalena, his nineteen-year-old wife, who possessed a fabulous soprano voice. When she sang, Bach must have felt young and confident. He would have enjoyed the feeling. Who wouldn't? She was bright, perceptive and responded quickly to the music he wrote.

Bach was already thirty-six, and knew that he didn't have many more years to live. Merely a year or so before, his beloved first wife Maria Barbara had died. She was just a few months older than he. Unlike him, most of her life had been spent bearing and rearing his children, many of whom had died young. Death came frequently, often unexpectedly, and Bach didn't want to die leaving so many ideas unexplored, unfinished.

Bach must have seen Anna first when she was a child of eleven or twelve perhaps, but even then she had the looks and voice. On his travels, Bach must have stopped many times in Wiessenfels and stayed with the Wilke family, for whom music meant a lot. He must have seen Anna Magdalena grow, and heard her sing, and coached her a bit. Perhaps that is why he didn't think twice to ask her to be his wife. It is true that he had a daughter and three young sons to look after, but I don't think that was the only reason, because Friedelena, Maria Barbara's sister who lived with the family, could have taken charge of the children.

Of course to forget Maria must not have been easy. Bach had been with Prince Leopold when he heard the terrible news of her death. He hurried back, but the funeral was over before he reached home. He only saw her grave. She was his cousin—a friend and a patient companion in his quest to make his name as Kapellmeister.

For the first few years of his life with Anna Magdalena, Bach must have felt unable to reconcile the grief and joy that gripped his heart. Reminders of Maria Barbara's presence were everywhere, the most potent of which was Catharina, his lovely daughter, who was only a few years younger than Anna Magdalena – a true copy of her mother.

*

I allowed Johann to finish his story, which he agreed was nothing more than speculation. But there was some semblance of truth in it. I didn't tell him if he was right or wrong. How could I have said anything? "Let him believe whatever he thinks is appropriate," I thought, but in one way he was probably right: Bach was truly in love when he composed those magical cello suites. In some, he celebrated his love for Anna; in others he grieved for Maria Barbara, dancing his courantes, menuets, bourrées, gavottes with both of them.

Before leaving, Johann asked me if I would let him take a few photos of the house and of my room. He looked surprised to see how small my bedroom-studio was. He saw the cello lying on the bed and took a few photos of me sitting with it. I don't know why he liked the armchair upholstered in the gaudy mauve fabric. He took a photo of the chair and of pipes tucked between two boxes of tobacco. He spent ten or so minutes finishing the job, and as he packed his camera and picked up his rucksack, I felt sad for a moment. I saw the little book of Goethe's poems on the shelf, picked it up and gave it to him as a small present. He took the book with both hands, bowed, turned to leave, stopped, turned back and asked if I would write something in it. I did. I don't remember the words exactly, but they were most probably about Bach and his God. I wanted to tell him that every little bit that Bach composed and performed was meant to reveal God's mystery; that occasions of joy and sorrow, love and grief were nothing but an excuse to exclaim His glory.

*

A few years ago I met a cute little girl on the beach. She was four or perhaps five, and I was surprised seeing her alone on the beach so early in the morning. For a moment I thought I glimpsed a hint of a little Martita in her: the same slow gait, the head bent to the left and the long hair tied with a yellow ribbon. "I wonder if she has Martita's eyes as well," I said to myself.

"What's your name?" I remember asking her.

"Juanita," she said, and smiled.

She was collecting shells.

"You like shells?" I asked her.

"Of course," she replied, and I felt silly that I had asked her. She said, "Do you want to have a look?" And without waiting for my response, she knelt on the sand and spread out everything she had collected.

"So many," I said, surprised. "And aren't they all beautiful?"

"Not all of them,' she said, and looked at me as if I had erred again. She pointed at those she thought were truly pretty.

They were pretty, and I didn't quite bring myself to ask her why. She touched each one of them, the pretty and the not-so-pretty, and sang a little ditty for each of them as if they were little creatures. Then she gathered them all, put them back in her little bag and resumed her search. I went with her, carefully watching her pick up this or that bit.

"Do you want me to carry your bag?" I asked her. "It must be heavy."

"No," she said.

"Why don't you leave behind the ones that are not so pretty?" I asked.

"No way, Grandpa," she replied, and this time the look on her face was hard to explain. Perhaps she was surprised and disappointed that the suggestion came from an old man like me.

*

Why was she so disappointed by my question? What was her secret?

Later that night I told the story to Martita, who mentioned that little Juanita was the granddaughter of the old carpenter who lived a few houses down the street.

"Is there a message for me in this somewhere, dear Martita?" I asked her.

"There certainly is," she said, and laughed.

All that evening and for many days I wondered about Juanita and what she had said to me. Because I was so eager to grasp the meaning, it remained out of reach. Then one morning as I got up to play Bach on the piano, a thought trickled in and lingered for a while. Here it is:

Because we find this or that thing so beautiful, we assume that it must have come into being at a special moment of inspiration or endeavour or because of divine benevolence. And that is why we love and cherish the moment. Yet perhaps this isn't quite true. Little Juanita loves her pretty and not-so-pretty shells equally. Doesn't she?

I walked out onto the terrace. The morning was unusually calm, and I was able to hear only two sounds: the music of Bach and the ceaseless rhythm of the sea.

Walter Benjamin's Pipe

"To the Cemetery?" she is asked. "No, not yet," she replies and requests to be taken to room number four. Her guide, a fifteen-year old boy, who introduces himself as Raul, leads her to the reception and talks to a middle-aged man with a black patch on his left eye. He is the manager. "Fermin," he calls out, and after a few minutes an old man, with a stooped back and no teeth, shuffles out of the back door.

"I know the room," Raul tells her, as they follow Fermin up the stairs.

Five years ago it was. Raul was just ten and a little scared to go inside. He shouldn't have been because he had been assisting his father for over three years by then, but this was a special and rather awkward situation: to measure the body of a dead foreigner. "Murder?" he remembers his mother asking his father. "Who knows," his father mumbled, "perhaps suicide or illness." "Santa Madre," his mother whispered, raised her right hand and crossed herself and then her lovely dark-eyed Raul. "Don't stay a minute longer than you have to," she warned him. He not only went inside but stayed there a few minutes longer than his father. "Come on Raul," his father called. He picked up the shiny object lying on the floor near the bed, put it in his pocket and scurried outside.

He didn't tell anyone about the object, not his mother and not even his good friend Pau. The German woman would be the first to see it. He would offer it for her to hold and notice her hand quiver (to touch or not to touch). Her anguished sigh, the look on her face, told him that it would be most appropriate to let her keep it.

"Take it, *por favor*," he says without any hesitation. '*Muchas gracias*,' she starts to reply but stops, embarrassed that the few phrases of Spanish or Catalan she knows won't be enough to express her gratitude.

The German woman's name is Margaret. Tall and thin, she has a sickly appearance. She must be as old as my grandmother, Raul thinks and is amazed when he learns she is just a year older than his mother. Next morning, walking with her up to the border, he asked her about the foreigner. "Was he a poet? Did she know him? Was he a relative? Why did he kill himself?"

Yes, why *did* he kill himself here? Why not earlier? In Berlin, Paris, Moscow or Ibiza? Georg had warned her. He knew Walter well. They all knew. Perhaps that is why, in Paris, when she was told that he was dead, her immediate response was: "Did he kill himself?"

She had left Berlin in the last week of September. Why then? Simply because to live amongst the ruins, without food, water and electricity, had become impossible. And then she remembered the brief note Georg had left for her. "Go and look for Walter," he pleaded. "Go immediately," he had added just below the signature. But she couldn't go immediately. The war was on.

It took her seven long days and nights to travel from Berlin to Paris. At times the train stopped for hours outside small stations, waiting to give way to the army convoys. It was late in the night when the train finally arrived at the Gare de l'Est. She spent the night at the station and in the morning walked four or five miles in the direction of the Jardin du Luxembourg. After reaching Boulevard Saint-Germain she decided to check the three addresses she had noted down in her diary. The first one was for the Maison Internationale de PEN on rue Francois Mion. The old man from whom she asked the way told her that she had already walked past the street that could have taken her there. The other two addresses were on the same street, and the street, rue de l'Odeon, wasn't very far, just a fifteen-minute walk at a leisurely pace. "Leisurely." She heard the word and wanted to smile, and the old man must have noticed her vain attempt to force it and said, "It's a beautiful day, so rare these days," and issued a loud but sickly laugh.

The late October day was truly glorious and for a few minutes she must have felt compelled to be happy. She stood at the carrefour and saw at the end of the street the heavy Corinthian columns of the theatre. She checked the numbers on the buildings: odd to her left and even to the right. According to her diary she should have walked first to number 12, rue de l'Odeon, the bookshop with the name Shakespeare & Co., but on the other side of the street was her third address, La Maison des Amis des Livres. She crossed the street, opened the door and heard the clock in the bookshop strike three. The bookshop was almost empty: an old man sat in the far corner of the room, reading a very large book resting on a table; a young woman stood near an office table talking to a woman sitting on the other side. She stopped at the door, then took a few reluctant steps and stopped again. The woman at the table, the owner perhaps, looked at her, and the younger, as if prompted, turned and glanced in her direction. She picked up a packet from the table, said goodbye to the woman sitting at the table and moved towards the door.

Now it was Margaret's turn. The woman at the table fitted the description perfectly: short and plumpish with blonde hair, dressed in a gown that reminded her of a nun's habit. The face, small and round, lit softly with a kind smile.

"My name is Margaret Stern," she said, "and I have come from Berlin. I am looking for Walter Benjamin." The words didn't come out easily. Her French was terrible and she was tired from the journey and the long walk. But there was another reason as well: the task she had been asked to perform was weighing heavily on her mind.

Adrienne introduced herself, shook her hand lightly and asked her to sit down. She spoke German and that helped her to feel at ease immediately. Margaret sat down, put her black handbag on the table, and then realising that it wasn't appropriate, grabbed it hurriedly and dropped it on the floor.

Adrienne asked her if she was an old friend of Walter's. She said no and added that she knew Georg, Walter's younger brother well. That was when Adrienne told her that Walter was dead, to which her response was "Suicide?"

"Perhaps, who knows?" Adrienne replied.

Margaret spent the evening and the next day in Paris with Adrienne from whom she heard about Port-Bou, the small Spanish town, where, in a Catholic cemetery Walter lay buried.

Hearing of his death, she could have walked out of the bookshop and caught the next train to Berlin. In Berlin she would have gone to Hilde, Georg's wife, and told her what she had found about Walter. The matter would then be formally settled. A job well done. A closure perhaps. But she didn't. Why? She herself didn't know the answer. What would Georg have done? He would have definitely gone in search of Walter, dead or alive. He was nineteen when he had volunteered to enlist in the war. Poor Walter was medically unfit for service and Georg, the next in line, had to step in.

"What are you going to do?" She heard Adrienne speak.

"Go to Port-Bou," she replied, surprised for a moment at what she had so unwittingly blurted out. Her answer to Adrienne's "Are you sure?" was simple: 'Yes,' She was grateful that Adrienne didn't ask her why because she didn't want to conjure an answer verging on a lie. She didn't have the time or will to think and hence didn't quite know the reason.

Her trip to Port-Bou was planned. She would catch a train to Narbonne and wait there for a train going to Spain. At Port-Vendress she would be met by Hélène, a local school teacher. She would spend the night with her and in the morning the two would cross the border by train and arrive at Port-Bou. Hélène was friends with a Catalan musician, a violinist, in the small port town, who, Margaret was assured, would assist them to find the hotel where Walter had been found.

"Hélène will look after you," Adrienne told her, but as it often happens, Hélène fell ill a few hours after she had welcomed Margaret at the Port-Vendres railway station. As a result Margaret had to travel on her own to Port-Bou. At the station she didn't have the patience to wait for the Catalan violinist and decided to find her own way to the hotel.

The train journey from Paris was long and torturous, mostly because she wasn't at peace with herself. She was troubled by the decision, the futility of the whole childish, and rather irrational, exercise. Reading wasn't much help. She should have brought something light and cheerful, although she did enjoy Walter's *One Way Street,* a collection of diary-like notes, some rather dense and heavy, but others light and intensely poetic. In Berlin Hilde had given her three pieces by Walter: a travelogue about

Naples published in the *Frankfurter Zeitung*; the booklet *One Way Street* and a typed copy of *A Berlin Chronicle*.

Margaret had spent most of her childhood in Berlin and perhaps that is why reading about the city pleased her. As she read, an old map of Berlin took shape in her memory. A strange map it was, an overlay of two sets of images: one of her childhood and the other of the city itself, imagined but very real. It pained her that most places so vividly described in the chronicle now lay in ruins, even the majestic and rather friendly lions on the gently sloping embankment of the Herkules Bridge. Like Walter, she too had sat on them as a child, firmly holding the hand of her mother. Now both were gone: the lions bombed and shattered and her mother gassed in one of the camps. So much death and yet she loves the city. Who doesn't? Georg did and he was sure Walter loved it even more. "We wanted to be Germans, you know," he told her once, and she felt that he was probably right: German and Jew with a comma in between. Perhaps that is why he would have wanted her to go in search of Walter: to find him and bring him home. Home? Can Berlin ever be a home to a Jew like her? "Why not?" Hilde had replied with a question. Yes, why not?

Margaret read *A Berlin Chronicle* and the *One Way Street* a number of times and slowly began to comprehend in them the presence of death's alluring shadow. There he is, reading an express letter received just that morning. The year is 1914 and the letter is from his young friend Fritz Heinle. "You'll find us lying in the Meeting House," Walter reads and rushes to the house immediately: the nineteen-year old poet is lying dead with Rika Seligson, his girlfriend. The story is simple but the tragedy most profound: they had turned the gas tap on to end their life, not because their love was impossible but because they were unable to live through the absurdity of a war that had just begun.

Walter must have also remembered his favourite aunt Friederike, his father's sister, who ended her life unable to fight depression. Gertrud, his cousin, a poet of considerable talent, was sent to the camps and killed. To imagine life without death is impossible, but death, unexpected, violent and tragic, must have become a *leitmotif* of Walter's life.

Did it worry him? Perhaps it did. Writing must have made its presence a little more companionable, but to tame its allure forever would have been impossible. "Don't be afraid, my friend," he must have heard it whisper. "Just call and I'll be there to help. Remember that it takes only a few minutes after which there is nothing but uninterrupted bliss." Yes, Walter, like her, must have known the little hunchback, who not only trips you, breaks your favourite toys and spills your soup but is ready to push you off the cliff. You have to keep on your guard, take precautions and be ready to shoo it off. She knows the trick; she too has fought the temptation, losing count of the times she had to reason herself out of the urge to jump in the Spree and drown. She failed once but was rescued by the two Gestapo men who had come to arrest her on a bright autumn evening in 1936. She was scared that she wouldn't be able to endure the torture and would betray her friends. She was right. The torture was relentless and the pain unbearable. Did she betray them?

She knew how dangerous it was to join the party, but she did, and was forced to bear the consequences. Simple.

So is this the reason she is going to Port-Bou?

Guilt, shame, a sense of duty or just fear. Why fear? Of what? Of herself perhaps? Of that moment when the expected suddenly becomes real and you begin to understand the mystery of life and death. And certainly hope, however illusory, that the knowledge so gained will at last bring a semblance of relief. She is going to Port-Bou to see for herself that precise setting—the customs-house, the police station, or perhaps the room in the hotel—that could have pushed Walter off the cliff. That he killed himself, she didn't doubt; she just wants to verify for herself that it only takes a trifle to convince oneself that the moment has come. A look in the mirror might be enough; your own face telling you that you can't go on any more, that the time is right for you to take the plunge. All sense of good and evil, just and unjust, beauty and ugliness, God or His absence are put aside. You are left with nothing but your own self, profoundly and desperately alone.

So is Walter a mere excuse? Surely it isn't so simple. Nothing ever is.

*

Unable to wait for the Catalan violinist she decides to walk up to the hotel. It takes her only five minutes to find Hotel de Francia. Many buildings on the way lie in ruins. The tall, three-storeyed hotel looks bleak; the peeled off paint uncovering patches of wet stone, the rusted metal railing on the balcony; windows shut, in a few the glass cracked or broken. She stands outside the hotel unable to make up her mind when a young boy asks her if she is in need of help.

"You must be German?" She hears him speak. The word "Deusher" alerts her. She is surprised but before she can ask him anything the boy opens a small bag and shows her a photo of Walter. "Yes, I have come to see his room," she tells him. The boy smiles, introduces himself as Raul and points to the door on the second floor. Attached to the door is a balcony with a railing. "Room number four," the boy announces, and she immediately understands that Walter must have stayed in that room.

In the afternoon the Catalan violinist will explain to her that the locals were already growing fond of Walter. A steady trickle of visitors from foreign lands wanting to see the hotel where a German poet was found dead convinced them that the dead poet was destined for posthumous fame. In no time a few turned themselves into guides eager to take the visitors around, telling them stories spiced up with rumours. The fact that the German poet was running from the Nazis added an element of mystique to the story, but the fact the escape failed so tragically made Walter a hero. They felt proud to claim a share of his fame, which, they were confident, would make one day their little town equally famous.

Room number four is unoccupied and Raul escorts her to the door. The old caretaker unlocks the door and walks away. Once inside she searches instinctively for a mirror and failing to find one looks at the bed, which she wonders isn't the same as the one in which Walter was found dead. She asks if she can open the door and step onto the balcony, but the door is locked. She wants to find out from Raul if from the balcony she would be able to see the bay and the sea, but gives up without trying. A silly idea suddenly creeps into her mind; she believes that if Walter had been able to get a glimpse of the sea from his room he would have been able to resist or at least delay the tragic moment.

The thought doesn't leave her and she walks with it silently to the cemetery, trying her best to add a degree of certainty to the idea.

She is with Raul and the Catalan violinist, who meets her near the entrance. "Miguel Sempre," he introduces himself. Later he will tell Margaret that he is an accountant and that music is just a hobby; that he enjoys playing and occasionally teaches violin in a music school. He will confess that he has only read a few minor things of Walter's but is very interested to learn more about him and his books.

The cemetery sits on top of a little hill sloping steeply towards the sea. From there she can see the bay, and across the bay, the road to Port-Vendres meandering through the humps. The sky is cloudless but for a few white streaks; the water in the bay still and almost quiet. Every now and then the wind blows and she hears the water splashing. The sea looks blank and she wishes for a boat with sails unfurled to appear from nowhere and add a fragment of hope. She is stunned by the beauty and thanks the locals for selecting such a nice place to bury their dead. That's when the thought, she had earlier called silly, intrudes again. No, it can't be true, she thinks, the beauty does possess power but the benevolence it is capable of bringing isn't boundless. Didn't Orpheus, too, lose the battle to bring Eurydice back? The music with which he mesmerised the goddess was profoundly beautiful but faced with death and his own doubts it failed, because it had to. Isn't this the ultimate lesson of the tragic story?

Miguel takes her and Raul to the niche of grave number one in the Catholic cemetery. "Walter was interred here," he tells her, "but last year in December the rental period ran out and he was removed to make way for Señora Francisca Costa Roset."

"Where is he now?" she asks him.

"You mean the remains?" Miguel speaks after a pause, "They are in the common grave, just there."

"So that's it then," she blurts out.

"Yes, Señora Margaret," Raul replies.

She says goodbye to Miguel at the railway station and after he has left asks Raul if he will take her to the walking track. She has made up her mind. Instead of catching the train back to Port-Vendres, she'll follow the track Walter had walked five years ago. She wants Raul to accompany her to the French border, from where she will make her own way on foot to Banyuls-sur-Mer and Port-Vendres. "No problems at all, Señora," Raul smiles and without any delay they start the walk. Raul knows the track. This is his third trip and he suspects that it won't be the last.

They walk for a couple of hours and reach the summit near the border. Raul leads and she follows. He is carrying her sleeping bag. He wanted the heavy back-pack as well but she refused. Before parting Raul gives her the tiny, stained-with-tobacco object and tells her that he found the penknife-like blade in room number four, the day he accompanied his father to measure the dead foreigner. The tiny thing is called a reamer; her father who used to smoke a pipe had something similar. He also used to have a small pick and a tamper.

She takes the reamer from Raul, opens her little purse to see if she can pay Raul some money to thank him for his help. She finds twenty francs and a few German marks. She gives him a few francs. He refuses to accept, but she insists, and he reluctantly takes the money and points in the direction of the track weaving down across the slopes. They hug; he kisses her on the cheeks and waits for her to pick up her sleeping bag, tie it to the side of the backpack, lift the two on her back and start walking. She walks for a few minutes and turns to look back. He is still standing at the same spot. She waves; he waves back and she turns round and continues walking.

It is already late in the evening and she doesn't want to get stranded on the track. She decides to walk faster but her feet resist. The hills are beautiful, the air light and fresh, and patches of the sea which intermittently become visible, lighten up her heart.

By the time she reaches a large clearing it is already dark. She is scared to go on walking. She pulls off her back-pack and realises that she is bursting. She squats near a bush and watched by a bird relieves herself.

She'll spend the night here, she resolves and starts looking for a suitable place to spread her sleeping bag. She finds two large boulders at the edge of the clearing and walks up to them. She likes their mute company. She doesn't mind being hungry but the thirst she feels annoys her and she scolds herself for being so careless.

Luckily the night is blissful and she is overwhelmed by these unforseen bursts of joy. The little crescent in the sky seems lonely and humble, jettisoned so arrogantly by a multitude of stars: right above her head the Little Bear with the Polar Star, and to its east the majestic Pegasus, and nearby the grand celestial river, the Milky Way. She looks and looks and then falls asleep.

The dream that lights up her sleep is rather strange. She is sitting in a boat stuck right in the middle of a large lake. From her boat she can't see the shore, which frightens her a little, but when she turns her head she finds Georg in the boat.

"I am sorry," she tells him.

"Don't be. It wasn't your fault," he replies.

"Did they torture you?"

"They couldn't help themselves. It was in their nature."

"And they killed you. Didn't they?"

"Yes, they did."

"So you didn't end your life."

"I didn't."

"But what about the power line? They say you grabbed the live line and killed yourself."

"Lies and more lies."

"I am sorry, Georg."

"I know you are, but they would have got to me anyway."

"But I wasn't careful. I should have destroyed the stupid article you translated."

"Yes, it was quite ordinary. Imagine losing life for such a shoddy piece of work; but tell me about Walter."

"Tell you what?"

"He is dead, isn't he? Did he kill himself?"

"I don't know. Perhaps he did. He had a bad heart as you know, and the walk must have drained him completely. He must have suffered a stroke."

"Yes, I knew about his bad heart. But he was lonely too. Very lonely. Born to live and die alone."

"No, I think he took morphine to ease the pain, but the pain wouldn't go, so he took more and more and then gave up. Just willed himself to die; it was the best option, he must have thought. But such an awful room to die in. Georg … where have you gone? Can you hear me?"

Margaret opens her eyes in the dream and looks. Georg has turned his back to her. She wants to get up, touch his shoulder and make him turn round, but she doesn't because the slightest move causes the boat to rock.

"I know about your mother," she hears Georg speak. "I saw her in the camp."

"'I was stupid," she tells him, "to think that I could have saved her. I shouldn't have told them anything."

She waits for him to say something: just "I know", "don't worry", "the times were bad". But he didn't say anything. "Please say something," she whispers and then begins to weep. With each loud howl her body shakes, the boat rocks and she finds herself in the water, drowning.

She wakes up. It is still dark.

*

In the morning Margaret gets up, walks to the little creek near the clearing and washes herself. She sits on a rock, opens her bag and finds half a bar of a chocolate. She eats it slowly and then kneels to wash her face and mouth. The little reamer slips out of her pocket and drops into the water. She jumps into the knee-deep water and searches for it with her hands, scouring the sandy mud and pebbles. After half an hour she gives up, drains the water from her shoes, changes her socks, packs her bag and walks away.

"I didn't deserve to keep it," she thinks. The thought makes her sad but she will survive the grief. "It is a trifle," she thinks, "compared to what I have been through."

He Likes Picasso but Loves Braque

Henri is getting late and this annoys him. He shouldn't have brought Claude with him today, he thinks, turns around to see what else Claude has found near the gutter or on the window of this or that house.

"Why can't he keep his mind focused?" He whinges all the time, upsetting Marthe.

"He is just six, Henri." She won't let him shout at the boy like this. "A child for God's sake."

He is a lovely boy, and to be honest Henri can't imagine life without him. When they walk together, Claude either skips ahead forgetting about his papa's crippled leg or lingers behind distracted by the most insignificant things.

He waits for Claude to look in his direction but Claude's eyes are fixed on the tree. Claude waves him back and Henri decides that it will be easier to return and see for himself the object that has caught Claude's attention. They both look and a little smile breaks on his face and lingers for more than a moment. The bird sitting on the branch of a leafless tree is wonderful: bright red bill, blue head, yellow-green collar and wings. "It's a lorikeet from Australia," he says. Claude wants to run home and fetch his mother but the crowd begins to build up. "It will be a magical spring this year," they hear someone speak. "Yes, it will be," a woman with a blue scarf consents.

They agree that this is the warmest February in many years. The sky is clouded but the rain doesn't stay for more than a few minutes and the drizzle itself is warm.

"Let's go," he calls Claude and to his surprise he runs ahead without a moment of hesitation. Henri walks behind still thinking about the bird. It must have escaped from a pet shop or one of the cages he has seen hanging in the balconies. An Australian lorikeet in Paris. He should go to the library, find an atlas and look for a map just to get a sense of the distance the bird must have traversed. It is too far, he knows, far too far.

But he doesn't know that Claude has hidden in his pocket a little feather fallen from the bird. Soon Claude will run inside the house and give the feather to Marcelle who, pleased with the unusual present will shower him with kisses. Marcelle loves him like her own son and both Henri and Marthe don't mind sharing Claude with her. She and Braque do need him.

For almost a year now, Henri has followed the same routine: daily at around eleven in the morning he walks to the Hotel Roma to say hello to Braque and Marcelle, and stays with them for a few hours. Often Marthe joins them around lunchtime carrying a basket with *roquefort* sandwiches, or her favourite *soupe au potiron*. Marcelle doesn't like her quiche and can't stand the raspberry macaroons either. However, Braque accepts everything Marthe brings and thanks her loudly and never forgets to kiss her tenderly.

As the lunch approaches some more visitors join them. Henri can't keep Braque any longer in the studio; to defy Marcelle's orders is beyond them. Their conversation has to stop.

Often Henri carries a camera with him. He likes taking photos. They help him to spot something new each time he looks at them. Why? He doesn't quite know. Maybe because the sharp contrast between black and white light enhances the shapes of things, making them more legible, even more desirable.

He should have taken a photo of the Australian lorikeet, he reprimands himself, conscious that the black and white film would have certainly failed to capture its splendour. His folding Kodak camera isn't suited to taking the photos he wants to, but it is small and easy to carry and what's more important not very expensive. Let Kahnweiler and Picasso tease him as much as they like. They are rich and famous. He has to be happy with what he can afford.

Braque's studio is on the top floor. Each time he makes his way up, the steps seem endless. It is often dark and he has to take care to avoid bumping into women carrying hot water. However the scene from Braque's balcony is most attractive. It makes him forget the trouble he takes to go up the steep stairway. Braque boasts like a child about the scene from the balcony and does not fail to point out to every new visitor the town of Argentuil, the place of his birth. For those who can't spot it well, he always has his binoculars ready.

A few weeks ago he saw Kahnweiler take several photos of Braque and Marcelle standing in the balcony. Kahnweiler loves his new toy and boasts shamelessly, not merely because it takes good photos. He got the photos printed and made Braque sign them. "Priceless documents for history," he said then hid them. Henri doesn't trust him.

But Braque is a dear friend and Henri believes that Braque too considers him a friend. In La Ruche they lived so close that it was possible to wave at each other from the window or shout a word or too, but now he has to walk at least once everyday to say hello and talk about this or that. As such their conversation happens without many words; just being with each other or looking at what each of them has done or half done, and exchanging a glance accompanied with "interesting", "that's nice" or "it works", are enough.

As a rule it is Braque who starts the conversation with the usual "How are you?" to which his reply is most of the time the same: "I'm very well, thanks, but not my arm, or eye or head." Strangely the left leg remains unmentioned, because they both know that it hurts and the pain isn't only physical.

In spite of the mundane nature of the conversation or the briefness of the time they spend together, Henri always comes out enlightened and as he walks back home in the evening, new ideas begin to take shape.

"I am learning," he says to Braque, Marthe and himself. He is only a couple of years younger than Braque, but has without any reservation adopted the role of a diligent student. He finds it amusing that Braque too envies his ability to make things Braque calls "solid"; things which so easily and naturally carve out their place in the surrounding space. The flatness of a canvas scares Braque, although he has never quite expressed it to Henri in that way, but the anxiety is far too clear to miss. That is why, Henri feels pleased that he can extend a helping hand, but whatever he says to Braque has to be forced out of him. "The best replies come to me late," he confesses to Marthe. She only smiles. What else can she do? She knows her Henri well: the slowness with which he does everything doesn't bother her much. Slow but steady and utterly reliable.

He is so very much like Braque, she can't stop saying to herself.

Picasso is different. She calls him a matador. She has seen him work; like Marcelle she has modelled for him. His fury intimidates her. A genius or a madman, she can't decide. Maybe both.

*

Henri is a true Parisian. He loves the city and hates travelling, mostly because of the continuous pain he suffers from. He likes the rare holiday trips he makes with Marthe and Claude but travelling tires him. Marthe understands his predicament and doesn't impose herself. She is happy to go alone with Claude and let Henri do his work in the back garden.

He is the son of a cooper and he too could have taken on the same trade but he seemed to have found working with stones and rocks more interesting. His father didn't object. It was a worthwhile trade after all. Wood or stone, Henri is confident, he would have one day turned to sculpting. It is hard to imagine carving tombstones, window sills and pavers his whole life.

He was eight, he remembers clearly, when Michel, his friend, took him to one of the ateliers of Rodin on Boulevard d'Italie. Michel's brother was an apprentice in the workshop. There he saw for the first time so many *Balzacs* lying around. He never met the great master in person but saw him walk past, give instructions, and even shout at young apprentices. The master had a terrible temper which Michel's brother had experienced first hand.

Perhaps that is the reason he didn't join the workshop, preferring instead Ecole Bernard Palissy, learning slowly the trade of an ornamental sculptor and stone carver. Monsieur Perrin's classes in the evening, however, weren't much help, although he did pick up the basic tricks of the trade.

And then he fell terribly ill. He was seventeen then. The tuberculosis

36

was so bad that the leg had to be amputated and the troubles didn't end there. In spite of many operations the pain remained. Lying in the bed, he must have dreamt many times of the great master's *Balzac* cooped in his robe, trying either to hide or free himself. That's the tension, he would realise much later, the tension of shapes entrenched inside slabs of rock and wood. The mind only feels their presence, the hands grope, almost in darkness, however solid the shapes might be. The enigma is in the arrival of the final shape, often quite different from what one had imagined. Perhaps that's what keeps one going: this subtle but certain displacement, a cleavage of a sort between the imagined and the real which ultimately reveals itself.

The amputation shocked him but it wasn't as profound or disturbing as the shock he experienced a few years later. He was married to Marthe by then and glad that she shared his enthusiasm for art and sculpting. One by one all the pieces he had sculpted were destroyed. "Just bad imitations of the great masters," he had called them. She tried to stop him but he had lost control. "Don't call them ugly," she had wanted to object. They weren't ugly, he agreed, but ordinary, unable to stir neither curiosity nor the desire to touch.

"I was astounded by the calmness with which you got rid of them," Marthe told him later. No fury, no regret, just a methodical destruction of pieces. But there was another reason: encounters with Picasso's Les *Demoiselles d'Avignon* and Braque's *Viaduct at L'Estaque*. Suddenly he felt the need to look at the things around him anew as if the little pieces he had made were blocking the view.

He didn't do much in the following few years, just watched his friend Braque and Picasso, who wasn't a friend, work. "I am not ready," he would tell Marthe, "still learning to look and see," he would add after a pause.

However to merely observe the world around him wasn't enough. He wanted to learn how to anticipate the moment when something novel, something truly magical, was about to reveal itself; to grow in himself that acute sense which would help him to be ready for it, so ready that the moment, however unexpected, wouldn't seem unexpected. He hadn't told Braque, but his daily meetings with Braque, he was convinced, were helping him move closer to this cherished objective. That's why he wasn't surprised when he saw the strips of brownish paper pasted on the canvas of Braque's *Head of a Woman* or when he looked the first time at Picasso's *Maquette for Guitar*. He just smiled to himself as if saying, he was waiting for it, and that he knew or perhaps could guess, what piece of marvel they would show him next.

And that's when he felt that he was ready to make his own things. "I am a sculptor," he said to himself. "Unlike them space isn't a problem for me. I know how to work with it."

*

So why is he so anxious today? Why this rush to see Braque? Didn't he talk to him yesterday or the day before? Yes, he did, and that precisely is the reason.

On the way to Braque, he had bought his *Le Martin* at the newsagent, stopped for a minute to read the headlines, rolled the paper back into his pocket and walked up the stairs.

"Quoi de neuf?" Braque as usual asked and he as usual passed him the newspaper without saying a word. The front page carried headlines of two murders: "Les Surprises De L'affaire Cadiou" and "Tu Dois Me Tromper", and squeezed in between the two: "Les Moeurs Anglaises". The first reported inconsistencies between the results of the autopsy on Dr. Cadiou's body and the type of bullet that might have killed him. However, both Braque and Henri were more interested in the second murder story and not only because the accused was Jose Forciganano, an Italian painter who had come to Paris from Buenos Aires where he had made quite an amount by selling second-rate paintings. Jose shot his wife Rosa Fernandez twice suspecting that she was having an affair. After shooting his wife he went to the concierge of the block and asked the police to be called to arrest him. He was duly arrested: the photo underneath the headline showed him being escorted by the police.

Intrigued by the words "Tu Dois Me Tromper" in double quotes and in italics they talked about what Jose Forciganano, the painter, would have spoken on his arrest. Whatever the reason, the headline was masterful. Were they addressed to the police or to his dead wife, who he was convinced had been betraying him?

Tu Dois: you must, you should, you owe: words taken out of context can mean anything, as do the objects, natural or made; they too change by the surroundings within which they find themselves. A guitar in a painting isn't a guitar you can play on, but the image of a guitar means something to us only because it's an image of an instrument with which we make music.

No, they didn't talk about anything of this sort; it wasn't in their nature to discuss abstract concepts. They were happier solving real problems of an artist's craft; for instance, how to find an appropriate place for this or that shape in a painting or *papiers colles*, or how to define the margins of visual space before transferring it to a canvas.

They talked for a while using as few words as possible and then Henri got up and drew a few lines on the wall. Braque watched him keenly. Henri added a few more lines: half circles, straight lines joining into a rectangle or a triangle; then Braque decided to move to the wall and shaded a few shapes in dark and grey, appended a set of fan-like shapes, which reminded Henri of the paper-planes he often made for Claude to fly. They moved back to their chairs and looked and smiled. The idea was beginning to take shape.

They heard Marcelle greeting Marthe and knew that soon they would have to go down for lunch. During the lunch they joked about St Bernard, Mme Lina Cavalieri's dog, who in a playful mood had overrun a tripe seller, knocking him down and injuring his right eye. The tripe seller sued the American operatic singer for large amount but the court only awarded him one twentieth of it and ordered him to pay a quarter of the costs for submitting an exaggerated claim.

After lunch Braque played a few songs on his accordion then they discussed his plan of a bike trip to Sorgues in June. The ride would take him close to a week, with overnight stops in Dijon, Macon and Cuthzon. An old atlas was pulled out and the route traced on the map. Marcelle didn't like the idea but to convince Braque to change his mind wasn't easy. She was going to remain in Paris organising their new apartment on Rue de'Abreuvoir, which needed more work to make it habitable.

Walking home with Marthe and Claude in the evening Henri kept thinking about the lines and shapes drawn on the wall. He didn't know then that in the coming six months he would turn the idea into a collage that he would call *The Dancer.*

At home that night he searched for his *Le Martin* and was reminded by Marthe that he had left the newspaper with Braque. He didn't tell her that he needed to look at the newspaper again, especially the words "Tu Dois". That night he couldn't sleep. To calm himself he decided to go to the back garden. He sat on the steps alone listening to the faint noises around him. He recalled that the front page of *Le Martin*, he had left with Braque, had a printing error; no, not an error exactly but a slight decolouring. The top half of the page, which included the masthead, was lighter than the darker yellowish lower half. As a result the italicised headline, marked by double quotes, stood out even stronger. At that very moment he also recalled the white canvas he had seen hanging on the wall of Braque's studio. Braque had cut a section from the front page of the news-journal Harve-Éclair and pinned it onto the blank canvas.

"So that's what it's going to be," he said and smiled. The revelation made him happy, and relieved, he returned to bed and slept the rest of the night undisturbed.

*

The following morning he is standing in the studio alongside Braque. Claude is in the kitchen with Marcelle. Henri can hear him talking to her. The boy can't control his excitement, and is eager to describe for her the Australian rainbow lorikeet he had seen a few minutes earlier in the street.

George doesn't ask Henri "What's new?" today, because the new is fixed in the corner, near the door, to the left of the blank canvas pinned with a strip from *Harve-Éclair.*

Inserted in the corner of the room, a meter or so above the floor, is a dark brown, almost black, triangular piece of cardboard, inclined slightly in the direction of the two viewers. Onto the plain surface of the cardboard, Braque has glued a number of objects made from paper. One of these strange things cuts through the surface and continues downward. There is bottle-like shape that reminds Henri of a wind instrument. Three cropped letters–A, R and T–are pasted on it.

The paper piece protruding below the cardboard stand carries a dark painted triangle with a horizontal strip underneath. The strip is printed with scale-like marks. A shape reminding Henri of a three-sided prism rests on the cardboard stand. The front of the prism is sliced open. It also carries the same scale-like marks. To the right of the three-sided prism, he spots a large L-shaped piece of white cardboard, the top right corner of which is folded in. That's where he finds the front page of his *Le Martin*. It is partially covered by the L-shaped cardboard. Only three letters–M, A, and T–are visible. The straight line under the masthead separates the words of the newspaper headline "Tu Dois".

Henri takes out his camera, moves a few steps back and takes three photos, one of which snaps part of the blank canvas with *Harve-Éclair* and a bunch of keys hanging from a hook near the door.

Henri doesn't ask Braque's permission to take photos. He doesn't need it. They both know it. The photos are important.

Braque's 'new thing' in the corner will begin to be called *The Corner Sculpture*. It will hang for less than a week in the corner and be seen by several visitors, one of which will be Tatlin, a young artist from Russia, who will one day become famous for his wonderful tower. After a few weeks Braque will destroy the sculpture and forget about it. Like all his other paper sculptures it will have done its job and disappear; only the photos taken by Henri will keep it alive.

*

On June 28, 1914 Braque began his bike-trip to Sorgues. Less than two months later the 'Great War' began and Braque was mobilised to serve in the army. He wasn't sent to the front immediately but joined the training camp in Lyon, from where he was dispatched to the western front at the Somme.

Picasso refused to enlist. "It's not my war," he argued, "let the French deal with it themselves." Kahnweiler escaped to safety in Switzerland.

Braque was caught in a hail of shells and rescued by stretcher-bearers. He suffered temporary loss of sight. Holes were drilled in his skull to relieve pressure but he survived the ordeal and returned to Paris, where Henri pulled out his camera again to take a few photos of Braque, sitting in a cane-chair; his head bandaged; he looks sick, broken and far too uneasy in the army overcoat.

The war changed everything. The close friendship between Braque and Picasso slowly dissipated, with profound consequences: nothing stylistically new is created by them, although Picasso soon became rich and very famous. Braque drifted out of sight.

Henri too would leave his obsession with geometrical shapes and angular lines behind, opting for smooth, soft and curved contours, so sensuous to touch. But he would never forget the moment when he first saw the paper sculpture in the corner of Braque's studio. However, when asked to think about the sculpture a little more he would say that the few minutes he had spent sitting on the steps in his back garden were perhaps more important, because that was when he had begun to anticipate the coming into being of the paper sculpture.

Anna and Fyodor in Basel

Another miserable day, Anna thinks as she steps out of the hotel to join her husband waiting on the street near the lamppost. He is holding an umbrella. The drizzle must have started just a few minutes ago. Should she go back to fetch her own umbrella? She looks at him and concludes that she can't keep him waiting any longer. He already appears irritated.

"Sorry," she says waiting for him to offer his arm. He does. They walk, she, as always, on his left. The umbrella is tilted to shield her from the rain and exposes his own right shoulder. He is getting wet and will catch cold, she thinks, but she can't do anything about it. They walk silently over the bridge, turn left and then right and soon find the building. As they climb up the steps and open the door the rain stops.

They both look tired; he from the journey—the train had arrived late because of a minor accident and the coach was cold; she from the journey as well as the pregnancy. At times she wonders how rapidly her life has changed. She met Fyodor Mikhailovich in October last year, to help him finish *The Gambler*. By December he had already proposed and she had accepted. The marriage took place in February and now she is pregnant. Three months have gone and the slight bump is already visible. The morning sickness troubles her but she doesn't worry Fyodor Mikhailovich with her problems. He has plenty of his own: debts, lovers, and the novel which he hasn't started writing but for which the publisher's advance has already been spent, mostly on gambling. She should have known that only a real gambler could write about gambling with such passion. Now it's too late. To deny that she feels intimidated by him would be dishonest. Physically he isn't big, just a few centimetres taller but he is older by almost twenty-five years and there is something strange about him, his face, particularly his eyes. She has tried to restrain the feeling of unease and at times she has almost succeeded, yet it returns again and again. Why does she call it unease? Why not fear? Fear, no she doesn't fear him; she wouldn't have married him if she did. Love? She wants to say it but the wretched word annoys her. How can one love such a man?

The first time she saw him he appeared quite old but then he started talking and his appearance changed. At the most thirty-five or thirty-seven, she thought, of medium height and build, always taking care to stand erect. Light chestnut-brown hair with a reddish tinge, pomaded and smoothed. His long thin face with full, untrimmed wavy beard merging with thick sideburns. Prominent nose, the crest slightly curved. A big forehead made larger because of the receding hair. Most striking of all were his eyes—both dark brown but the right distinctly different, the pupil enlarged, filling the whole eye, its iris almost invisible. The uncanny, at times, mysterious look was caused by this distortion. She remembers him telling her about the injury. During an epileptic attack he had lost balance and fallen on a sharp object and hurt his eye. The drops recommended by Professor Yunge had healed the wound but the pupil remained enlarged.

The pale almost sickly face had made Anna's heart crumble. He appeared weak and vulnerable. To look after the sick soul of a great writer, Anna thought then, she must find a way to love him.

The first fit she witnessed, although it happened just a few weeks after her marriage, strengthened her resolve. "Yes, he needs my love," she decided there and then.

She hates his gambling but feels more anxious about the fits; try as hard as she may she still hasn't got used to the certainty of the crippling attacks. But she isn't going to give up, she often tells herself; she'll not only learn to read the signs of an impending fit but find a way to shield him from the possible causes and hence protect him from further damage. That is why she has mixed feelings about the visit to the gallery.

He had been told about the painting in Dresden and once he was reminded that Karamzin, the famous historian, had praised the painting in his travel accounts, he decided that he would have to see it. But why is she so anxious about the encounter? What could be so alarming in the painting? She should just relax, she tells herself, as they climb up the stairs to reach the hall with Holbein's paintings.

They don't have to look for it. It's right there as if waiting just for them, hanging on the narrower side wall, alone because of its odd shape—long and narrow, almost of the size of a coffin for a tallish man. *The Body of the Dead Christ in the Tomb*, she would whisper to herself later walking back to the hotel but now in the gallery there in no time to read the caption because she has to keep an eye on her dear Fedya looking at the painting. "Are you alright," she wants to ask but doesn't because he isn't. Not at all. Suddenly she herself feels sick, ready to throw up. She rushes out into the adjoining hall, finds a chair near the window and sits down. The window has been left open, just a little. She listens—to the horses trotting past, a man running followed by a scream then a flutter of wings; she looks outside and sees a flock of white pigeons taking off from a tree on the river bank and landing on the ground near a bench where an old woman is sitting with a small bag. She should go back, she thinks and after the old woman finishes feeding the pigeons she does.

Fedya is still standing in front of the painting. He hasn't moved at all; hasn't even noticed her rushing out and coming back. He is lost. The symptoms are clear. The pale sick face looks sicker than ever—dread, horror, panic and perhaps awe. He seems to be clamped down, almost dead. She looks intuitively at his right eye and decides what she has to do. She takes his arm and pulls him gently away. He gives in. She escorts him to the adjoining hall and makes him sit on the chair near the window. Luckily there is no one else in the gallery. Please don't be sick, she pleads silently, not now. She repeats the words like a prayer hoping to deter or at least defer the fit till they are back in the hotel room. Minutes pass. She notices that the woman outside is still sitting on the bench surrounded by the pigeons. A boat with a white sail appears on the river; someone walks with an accordion playing an almost familiar tune. Her husband turns to look outside. After a minute or so he turns back and she finds a smile on his face. "I am alright dear," he whispers, "it won't happen. Let's go home." He gets up holding her arm and they walk down the steps.

At the gate he looks at her again. The smile reappears. He is calm now; asks her to stop, looks at her and says that he would like to go back to see the painting. "No Dear Fedya," she wants to say. Luckily he notices the agony on her face and, convinced that she won't allow it, relents. "Let's go to our room," he says and they walk out of the gallery.

It would be nice to go to Geneva, she thinks as they stroll back to their room, and feel settled for a few months. She misses the daily routine anchored firmly to his working hours. He likes to work at night and often writes till the early hours of the morning, gets up late, never before eleven. They have a quick breakfast after which she goes out for a stroll as recommended by the doctor. He continues to work and at three or so they go to a restaurant for a meal, after which he walks her back to the apartment and goes to a café or a library to read Russian and foreign newspapers and magazines. The evenings are meant for taking dictation from him. She sits with the typewriter and he paces up and down. At night he checks the typed material, edits, reads books and takes notes. She likes the discipline and gets annoyed when the routine is upset. She wants to work, for him and with him—to become an integral part of his writing life. A proper wife and partner of a writer, not a mere housewife. And he never hesitates to acknowledge her assistance. Without her, he would be lost, he has told her several times, forgetting that she is only twenty. She feels proud of herself and him.

*

He has told her about the new novel and is surprised by the effort he has made to get it right. With *The Gambler* it was different. The book was ready when she had started taking dictation. She was amazed by the intensity with which words poured out of him, perfect in shape and meaning, requiring hardly any alteration.

With this yet to be written novel, she is witnessing something entirely different. He doesn't appear so sure; maybe that's what fascinates her more than anything else. She knows that in the end it will work itself out, but the magic and the mystery associated with the process of searching, guessing, writing and then trashing all that had been written, intrigues her.

He has told her that he wants to write a novel with a positive hero, a sort of Christ-Prince, wise but innocent like a child, so pristine and unblemished that people around him are ready to believe that he is a freak, a fool perhaps, an idiot. She notices the interest with which he is reading *The Life of Jesus*. He praises the book, its style and content, and she is pleased that he likes the book.

Almost daily he brings her stories from the Russian newspapers, and because some of them enter his notebooks, she suspects that some of them might one day appear in the novel. In the notebook she finds newspaper reports of two trials: one that of Mazurin, a rich Moscow merchant, who was arrested for killing a well-known jeweller. The body was found buried in the basement of Mazurin's palatial home. The second trial involves a fifteen-year old girl. Her name is Olga Umetskaya. She is the step-daughter of a famous landlord and has been charged with trying to kill her father by setting ablaze his country house. The reports describe repeated abuse of the girl, involving sex, prostitution and other sordid acts.

They talk about the trials, especially that of Olga and she doesn't fail to observe that Fyodor Mikhailovich is both fascinated and disturbed by it. She reads his brief comments such as, 'interesting', 'can be used', 'find out more' and waits eagerly for new additions in his diary.

Back in the hotel she wants to ask her dear Fedya about the painting but doesn't. "I can't," she tells herself, "he still looks tired and sick." But she is more anxious to know than ever, because only then can she prepare herself for an impending fit. She has witnessed how they leave him terribly weak. For days after the fit, he feels drained of energy unable to read or write. From where does he find the desire and will to commence writing, she wonders all the time.

*

On the train to Geneva, she finds the courage to ask him about Holbein's Christ. From the lengthy pause that precedes the answer she surmises that her dear Fedya hasn't quite recovered from the shock. He tells her that Holbein painted the Christ in 1521 but was forced to change it a year after; that as a Holy Sepulchre, the painting was meant to remain concealed behind a painted panel, revealed to the congregation only for three days following the Black Friday; that a German by the name of Matthias Grunewald had also painted something similar ten or so years earlier; it was called *The Lamentation of Christ,* but Grunewald's Christ, he insists, contrary to what others believe, is very different from that of Holbein's. Still waiting for the right answer she asks him if it was appropriate to show Holbein's Christ in a gallery. The smile on his face assures her that he has understood the real intent of her veiled query and that he isn't really ignoring her question. From the words that follow she concludes that Fedya is disturbed by two very specific features in Holbein's wonderful painting—the soiled white shroud and the sharp curved wound just below Christ's right rib.

"So utterly dead," he tells her, "so complete and final, that the possibility of resurrection seems nothing but an illusion."

But why doesn't a dead Christ on the cross in a church disturb us, she asks herself. Is it because of the holy awe and wonder we feel in a church? The dead Christ inspires faith and the hope we need because only through hope we learn how to endure life. However, this short conversation doesn't satisfy her. She wants to know more about his response to the painting but her desire is thwarted by her concern not to disturb him more and she allows the conversation to be superseded by mundane talk about the weather, meals and money.

The unanswered question remains suspended waiting for the right moment which arrives in Vevey, a small town on the eastern shore of Lake Geneva. The stay in Geneva brings them joy then grief. Their daughter, Sophia, named after Fyodor Mikhailovich's favourite niece and also, as Anna firmly believes, after Sonya Marmaledova, the beautiful but unfortunate saviour in *Crime and Punishment,* is born. She dies three months later, making their escape from Geneva inevitable.

*

One night in Vivey, Fyodor Mikhailovich dictates "… they went through the rooms, the Prince had already walked; Rogozhin walked ahead followed by the Prince. They entered a large hall. Here on the walls hung several paintings—portraits of bishops and some landscapes on which it was rather hard to see anything. Above the door to the adjoining room hung a painting of a rather queer shape ....."

Here it comes, Anna thinks before Fedya is able to finish the long sentence, the dead Christ of Holbein, and she is right. The exchange between Rogozhin and the Prince makes her heart jump. In a flash she recognises that Fedya has found the most fitting place for the painting in the novel—the bleak house where Rogozhin will one day kill the beautiful Nastasiya Philippovna and escort the Prince to show him her dead body. There beside the bed the police will find them both—the killer and the idiot Prince, in shock and insane.

Its second appearance in the novel doesn't surprise her that much. Is this because she is bored by the unbelievably long and cumbersome confession of Hippolyte? The presence of this young boy, passionate and pitiful, fighting the fatal illness, appears to her superfluous in the story. But she doesn't ask him to do away with Hipployte or tone down his voice, because in Hippolyte's confession she finds the answer to the question she had not so long ago asked Fyodor Mikhailovich. That day in the train to Geneva, the question, she knows, wasn't ignored but the answer was tactfully postponed.

"I love these moments of metamorphoses," she ponders for days afterwards, when life outside the story enters the story, transforming itself and the story as well. She calls these moments magical and cherishes their presence, feeling proud and even blessed that she has got the opportunity to witness their arrival and to live so close to them.

Living with Fyodor Mikhailovich has made her more alert to the world around her. However, this doesn't mean that she was less observant or careful before she had met him. She has noticed that often walking through an exhibition of antique pieces of porcelain in a gallery or a shop, one or the other piece forces her to stop, look and touch. When she walks away the object calls her back forcing her to return to have another look. The piece entraps her, but often it's the human hand she imagines fashioning the piece into existence that fills her heart with joy and sadness.

Why sadness? She has always wondered, but only now, living with her Dear Fedya, sharing his joys and sorrows, she has come to realise how transient true beauty is.

She knows that Fyodor Mikhailovich often jokes about her passion for antique porcelain and pottery, but she also knows that he respects the seriousness with which she maintains her interest in pottery. When he has time he asks her to read some of her descriptions from several of her neatly labelled notebooks. Her descriptions are precisely illustrated with sketches and stories on the provenance and history of this or that piece. She is proud of his interest in her work, which he knows isn't merely a hobby.

She remembers clearly the beautiful Chinese vase that used to sit on the table near the window of his study in St. Petersburg. There wasn't anything special about the vase but somehow it's the vase that keeps the memory of her first few working days with him alive. There he is, standing in the corner, measuring the shape of a forming sentence as she waits with a pencil in her hand. The sentence doesn't arrive and she looks up and to avoid looking at him directly, she locates the vase to distract her attention. She finds the vase perfect in size, shape and colour, and feels as if it was meant to be there, waiting for her to cast its becalming glance in her direction and tell her that she shouldn't worry about him or herself, and that she should let the moment flow and follow its natural course.

A few weeks later the vase disappeared and it didn't escape Fyodor Mikhailovich's attention that Anna was looking for it. "He is embarrassed," she thought and didn't want to trouble him by inquiring about it, but somehow she wasn't able to control herself. "What happened to the vase?" She asked. "Did it break …?"

He didn't reply immediately and she was relieved that it wasn't broken only pawned to fetch twenty-five roubles. That a few roubles from the money so acquired went to pay for her services, made her sad.

A year or so later she did witness Fyodor Mikhailovich breaking *her* beautiful Chinese vase. Not physically but in the story he was dictating. That she was able to anticipate the precise moment pleased her a lot. Like co-conspirators they enjoyed the moment and acknowledged the joy with smiles. The Chinese vase was retrieved from the pawn shop and restored, then broken by the idiot prince. The setting too was perfect—the sitting room of General Epanchin, whose wife and three beautiful daughters witnessed the unwieldy confession made by the Prince. He was agitated, overwhelmed by the occasion. The four women waited impatiently for something untoward to happen and it did. He knocked the vase off the table and it broke.

*

"Why is the idiot prince called Lev Nikolaevich?" Anna often wonders. She regrets that she didn't ask Fyodor Mikhailovich while he was still alive. Every time she picks up a book by Graf Lev Nikolaevich Tolstoy, she thinks about the two names.

"Just a coincidence," she tells herself, but knowing that her dear Fedya was a clever trickster, she smiles and laughs, enjoying the moment of her strange discovery.

That the two, dear Fedya and Graf Tolstoy, never met, amazes her. They should have, she thinks and tries in her imagination to create such a moment, but fails.

She also thinks of the days after her dear Fedya's death. She had waited for a brief note from the great writer expressing grief for her loss, but nothing had come from him. Nothing at all.

But she was wrong. A note did arrive from Graf Tolstoy, addressed, however, not to her but to Nikolai Strakhov, the literary critic and a friend. She thanked Strakhov for passing on the note to her, calling it a wonderful tribute to Fyodor Mikhailovich.

But one sad thought never leaves her mind, and although she will try to find an adequate explanation, the sadness will gnaw at her heart. Only once would she find the right words to express it and that too because Lyuba, her daughter, wouldn't stop pestering her.

"We returned from Europe after three years," she told Lyuba one night.

"Not three but three and a half," Lyuba corrected her.

"And I got busy with the household and the business of selling your Papa's books."

"That was good, wasn't it?"

"Yes, it was, but it took away from me the thing I treasured most." And before Lyuba could say anything she added, "the moment when he turned words into stories, letting me peep inside his heart, mind and soul."

The Last Smile of Graf Tolstoy

I can picture the scene vividly, almost like a fresh print of a photo—there she is, my Babushka Sofiya, a mere five-year old girl then, standing up on her toes near a large window, looking inside; both her hands raised up to her face and cupping it to shield her from the bright early-morning sunlight, and thus help her see better. There is no one else in the photo; the snow is everywhere and the window frame stands out a like a dark apparition.

Every time I recall the image, I want the five-year old Sofiya to take her face from the window, turn and look at me. Why? Just to check if she was as pretty then as she always was, even when she was a frail old woman of ninety.

She died two years ago, the day I saw Yeltsin standing on the top of an army tank, heralding the end of the coup and of the Soviet Union. Our whole life changed that moment. The freedom he promised was short and chaotic from which the only way out was to return to the same old pattern of command and obey. The system didn't change, the rulers did. Some became very rich overnight but most lost everything they had managed to save. Like me. I sound bitter, don't I? But I can't help it. "Be patient my dear," Babushka Sofiya, would have definitely said. Yes, she knew the wisdom of patience.

Like my mother and me she was also a teacher. She taught geography, but I doubt if she loved maps the way I do. I collect them with passion but not because I am a collector of rare or, as they say, collectable items, but because they let me walk the places I only dream about. I like the physical or topographical maps in particular because they allow me to imagine the landscape. Recently a friend at the university showed me some aerial photographs of the Moscow region. He calls them stereo-pairs because they are photographed as pairs. To look at them, one needs a stereoscope, which adds depth to the otherwise flat surface. That day I saw lakes and ponds, creeks and rivers and straddling along the margins mounds and hillocks sloping gently up and down. There were sharp cliffs along the banks and breaking through the cracks streams of water. But most enchanting of all were the pine groves interspersed with birches and oaks. The photos were black and white and yet I was able to recreate in my imagination most of the missing colours and tones. It felt as if I had turned into a bird flying freely over the painted landscapes of my favourites, Levitan and Shiskhin. The forest smelt, sending wafts of spicy, almost tangy, air. I wanted to lie down on the wet ground, and seep into the cracks, like water leaking from the snow melting slowly.

Babushka Sofiya loved this land more than I could ever dare to imagine. "I have my own Doctor Astrov in me," she would often say, reminding me how much she adored her Chekhov and his *Uncle Vanya*.

*

Many years ago, Babushka Sofiya took me to see her little village. I was eight then, and the year was 1953, the year the great dictator disappeared from our life forever.

We boarded a train one Saturday morning in July at the Kurskaya Station and travelled past Tula, then Shchekino, and changed to a train going east at a junction the name of which I don't remember. We got off the train at a very small station. We walked outside and Babushka asked Astap, a peasant, to give us a ride to her village Vishenki. He was much older than Babushka and had known her as a child and remembered her father, from whom he had learnt to read, write and count.

"I wasn't good with books at all," he told me and laughed and then coughed for a long time.

"Getting old," he complained and laughed again. On the way he and Babushka talked about the village, the famine, the war, and 'dear old Graf Tolstoy'.

For the first hour in the train I kept asking Babushka to tell me stories but then fell asleep. Babushka woke me at Tula and I was quite angry with her that she didn't keep her promise to wake me to see our beautiful Oka.

"Don't worry, my Darling," Babushka said, "you'll see it when we go back, and if not on this trip then on the next; you have years and years to live and the Oka isn't going to run away." As it turned out I missed my beautiful river on our journey back as well.

"Never mind," I must have said, "it's just a river."

I didn't know then that my little Alyosha would catch his first fish in the same river and a year after my dear Sasha would breathe his last there as well. He drowned you know, fell through a hole in the frozen river and was carried by the current downstream. By the time the divers from the nearby kolkhoz arrived it was already late. Little Alyosha, my poor darling, was with him that morning. To this day he blames himself for the accident. He is silly. He shouldn't. Alyosha didn't go near a fishing rod after that. Gave up altogether. "That's good," I tell him. I don't like fishing at all; imagine catching the poor things for fun, torturing them and then throwing them back, assuming that they would happily swim back to life; most of them perhaps do but many I suspect must remember the pain. Who wouldn't?

Alyosha lives in Irkutsk these days, with Lena, his motherless daughter. He is an artist and paints wonderful landscapes. But enough about him. He can tell his own story himself.

The old *izba*, in which Babushka Sofiya was born, wasn't there any more. In fact only very little of the original small village had survived—a few very old houses scattered on the bend of a little river called Gushina Rysa. The river, to be honest, wasn't a proper river; more a series of isolated ponds overgrown with duckweed, linked together occasionally during the floods brought by the thawing snow or the summer rain. Babushka appeared disappointed. As a little girl she used to swim in it, she would repeat again and again, trying in vain to convince me. She shouldn't have. I believed every single thing she used to tell me those days. We didn't spend more than a day in the village that time, but since then I have visited the site many times, often with my year-six students who have decided to look after the little river of Babushka Sofiya.

On our trip back we waited for the train at the station and Babushka showed me the old house of the stationmaster, the house where Graf Tolstoy had died many years earlier.

*

I turned fifty last year. Alyosha wanted to arrange a large party but changed his mind because he didn't want to upset me. He knows that I still miss Babushka Sofiya and although she died peacefully in her sleep, her absence still haunts me. "I wasn't there," I say to myself, "when she needed me most." But it wasn't entirely my fault. I had asked her many times to move in with me, but she wouldn't listen. "Moscow isn't for me," she'd often say, "so noisy, so busy." She loved living alone in her dacha surrounded by trees, birds and sunflowers. I agree it would have been quite hard for her, trapped most of the time on the eighth floor of our ugly building.

I got the call in the afternoon. Vanya, her neighbour, was on the phone. He told me that his wife Varya had found Babushka in the morning sitting in her reading chair, still wearing her glasses, with Marusya, the cat, asleep on the windowsill. By the time I arrived at the dacha she was lying washed and dressed in the coffin, her two war medals pinned on a little cushion placed on her side. She looked so beautiful in the fading light of the day. Like a face painted on an icon, her face glowed. It seemed so miraculous that it took me a while to bring myself to kiss her.

Why was she so beautiful? Is this because she lived her life with grace and humility? Even the way she died, alone but without any fuss, is remarkable. Her main preoccupation was never to hurt anyone or be someone else's proxy to inflict pain on others. Maybe that's what helped her remain sane and sensible. Think for a moment of the ordeals she went through—revolution, civil war, famine, purges, the war again, more purges and the collapse in 1990. The upheavals of her own life were equally tragic. Deaths and more deaths—parents, husband, lovers, her only daughter. And yet she survived. "We all do," she would have answered, "we have to."

Searching through her things after her death I was surprised by the absence of things we usually call special; there weren't any cherished photos, albums, souvenirs or mementos. "I don't need them," I remember her saying to me. "If I can't keep memory of this or that it in my mind, it means I don't want to or need to remember it." I suppose that is why her own memory was so capacious, so unbelievably reliable.

But there were notebooks, dozens of them, neatly written, carefully dated, signed and often illustrated with sketches. The text was simple, often a list of things or events and one liners such as: *It rained today the whole day; there is no food in the house; mama is ill; Her name is Olya; Aleksei hasn't replied; I like Mayakovsky* (underneath a few lines from one of his poems); *the young man who played violin in the tram was blind; when I am twenty I'll catch a train to Vladivostok, board a ship to the island of Hawaii and watch hot lava pour and tumble into the sea.*

Like the text in the diaries, sparse and rather perfunctory, her other possessions were few and basic. She wasn't frugal or miserly, but she was always very choosy in whatever she bought or kept. Her needs were elementary and to crave for something wasn't in her nature. I wish I could have inherited just a bit more of her discipline, of her eye for the beautiful and of her precision to decide what and how much of this or that was enough for her. She loved books but kept only those which she really liked. There was a time when one could buy the complete editions of her favourite authors—thirty volumes of one and twenty-five of the other, all perfectly bound, to sit neat and tidy in the bookshelf in a room. No, she avoided that type of trap. She preferred two or a maximum of three books by her favourite writers. Many years ago when I fell in love with Chekhov, I read each and every book of his, including all his letters. Babushka Sofiya was very different. Of Chekhov, she had only one, of Bulgakov two, and of her favourite, Tolstoy, just three, neither *War and Peace* nor *Anna Karenina* but three collections of novellas and stories: *The Cossacks, Kreutzer Sonata* and *Childhood.*

I was pleased that there wasn't any clutter left for me to sort and get rid of. I knew each and every bit, its provenance and its significance. But then something rather strange and mysterious suddenly showed itself.

*

Lena, my little darling, found it in one of Babushka Sofiya's old bags.

Alyosha had left Lena with me to spend the winter months. In the last winter she caught pneumonia and Alyosha didn't want her to suffer again. She is twelve now and plays the violin well. I was pleased to have her. Once a week I took her to Moscow for her lessons in the music school. We went to a few concerts in the Tchaikovsky Hall and were lucky to hear and watch *Boris Godunov* in the Bolshoi.

In the morning that day I had gone to check on Varya. Her husband had died the year before and she wasn't keeping well, counting her own days. I have rarely seen someone so keen to die.

When I returned in the afternoon I saw Lena sitting with a bag. "Look, what I have found," she said, and began to undo a packet wrapped in a few sheets of yellowed newspaper. Inside the packet in a linen bag were a pair of peasant shoes. The sole of the left shoe was cracked but both were neat and clean. There was a small hand-written tag tied to the other shoe. I looked at the tag and read: *The Shoes of Graf Tolstoy, year 1880.*

The packet also contained an envelope with three black and white photos one of which looked familiar. It showed a little girl standing near a window of a house and looking inside. The uncanny similarity between the photo and the scene I had so often imagined startled me at first. "I must have seen this photo," I thought, "Babushka Sofiya must have shown it to me. Yes, she certainly must have."

"Is that you, Babushka?" Lena asked

"Not me my darling," I said, "but Babushka Sofiya."

"Who is Babushka Sofiya?"

"She is my Babushka."

"But she looks so much like you."

"Not really. You can't see the face of the girl in the photo."

"I know I can't but I am sure she has your face."

"How can you be so sure?"

"I just am," she said and smiled.

That evening before going to bed, I told Lena the little story about Graf Tolstoy, which Babushka Sofiya used to tell me when I was Lena's age.

It was very early in the morning, and the morning was cold but the sky clear, lighted so very slightly by the moon. I ran out of the izba and saw hundreds of people crowded near the house of the stationmaster. An old lady, hysterical and angry, paced to and fro outside. Then she went in and most of the crowd rushed to the door. I wanted to know what was happening inside and went to the window to look and that's what I saw— on the bed lay and old man, sick and tired, his face very similar to that of Christ; the head resting on a raised pillow, the eyes shut; the beard almost as white as that of a Ded Moroz; two large fingers of the right hand rested on his chest. Then he opened his eyes and turned his head and saw me looking at him. He did see me; I am sure because he smiled and for a moment his face glowed, the fingers quivered as if he was trying to lift his hand and wave; but he didn't and then the smile disappeared. He was dead. Soon I heard my father call and I was taken away from the window.

In the morning Lena asked me if it was a true story. "I think it is," I told her and showed her Babushka's Sofiya's note in one of the diaries. It was a short note that read: *When I was five I saw one morning Graf Tolstoy die but before dying he looked at me and smiled. I still remember his smile.* The date underneath the note was 16th May, 1945.

*

I didn't mention to Lena that I had heard from Babushka Sofiya several versions of the same story. The difference was in the way it was embellished a little each time but what remained unchanged was one particular sentence, and every time she uttered the words, *I still remember his smile*, her face would turn mysteriously beautiful.

"So is the photo real?" Lena wanted to know. "Is the girl in the photo really Babushka Sofiya?" She must be, otherwise why should she keep the photo. However, what I wanted to know most myself was the name of the person who had taken little Sofiya's photo.

A year after Babushka Sofiya's death, I went to the Tolstoy Museum in Moscow to make some inquiries. While Babushka Sofiya was alive the idea hadn't crossed my mind. She was not only my Babushka, but also my 'real' mother, and I didn't have any desire to doubt her.

I also didn't forget my trip to Vishenki with her, the village in which she was born, but somehow I must have stopped thinking about it. Then one day in the late seventies, when I began teaching in the high school I suddenly decided to visit the village again. Just to see if my pupils would find it interesting to work in the region. I persuaded Babushka Sofiya to come with me and we visited the village a number of times. On each of our trips we stopped at the railway station of Astapova and spent some time in the stationmaster's house, which was now restored and turned into a proper museum. We would sit outside on the bench. Babushka Sofiya would ask me to get her a cone of chocolate ice-cream and eat and smile. After finishing the ice-cream she would get up, walk to the window and look inside. One of the woman-guides in the museum found the ritual mysterious and wanted to know more, but Babushka refused to talk to her.

In the museum in Moscow, I was able to find more about Graf Tolstoy's final days in the stationmaster's house in Astapova. I saw his photos, heard his voice and even watched a short film. Monsieur Pathe, a famous newsreel man of the day, had ordered his cameraman to record the events unfolding at the railway station. His cameraman Meyer was given clear instructions—*try to get as many close-ups as possible, film the name of the station, the family members (particularly his wife), the coach and the house in which the Graf was sleeping; don't forget other famous ladies and gentlemen in the crowd.*

There was a short sequence in the film that showed Sofiya Andreevna, Graf Tolstoy's wife, pacing up and down outside the house. Often she would stop at the window and look inside and then walk away. She looked distressed, even wept. For a moment the camera turned in the direction of the crowd and I saw a little girl, walking with a man holding her hand. They were walking away from the camera and it was hard to ascertain if the little girl was indeed little Sofiya.

On one of my subsequent visits to the museum I took 'Graf Tolstoy's Shoes' with me to show them to Ivan Sergeivich, one of the curators. He was, as expected, surprised and asked me if I would leave the pair with him for a few days. He wanted to make some inquiries and show the shoes to other curators in the Tolstoy Museum at Yasnaya Polyana. He promised that he would phone me in a few weeks.

I didn't hear anything for him for three or four months. In the winter when Lena once again came to Moscow to live with me, we decided that we should phone him. Luckily we didn't have to phone because soon a short letter arrived in which Ivan Sergeivich invited me to come to the museum.

Ivan Sergeivich apologised for taking so long to respond to my queries about Graf Tolstoy's Shoes. He had been kept busy with some urgent family matters at home. I noticed that he coughed a lot and appeared unusually pale. I felt sorry for him. He was indeed a kind man.

Soon he took us to his little office and there on a desk near the window I saw two pairs of peasant shoes. He switched on the table lamp and asked if we knew which of the pairs was brought in by us. Neither Lena nor I could spot any difference between the two. The tag that Babushka Sofiya must have fastened to 'her' pair of shoes wasn't there any more.

He turned the pairs over to show us the soles and the difference between the two was immediately clear. The tacks in the sole of one of the shoes were not lined up properly; some were driven in too hard and flattened and the other hadn't gone in straight. In comparison, the other pair looked neatly finished.

"These are yours," he said pointing at the pair with a neat finish. "Lev Nikolaevich, you know," he added after a pause, "wasn't very good at making shoes."

"I hope you aren't disappointed," he said handing me a few pages he had photocopied from a book of reminiscences published by Ilya Tolstoy, Lev Tolstoy's second son. I brought the pages home to read. But before we left, Ivan Sergeivich asked us about Babushka Sofiya. I obliged. He heard me patiently, didn't interrupt me once and didn't take any notes. Just listened.

"You know Anna Ivanovna," he told me after I had finished, "the shoes your Babushka Sofiya kept were most probably made by her father, who as you tell me was a teacher in a village school. He must have been a keen disciple of Graf Tolstoy, striving to emulate everything the great man said or did. But he was, I am sure, a better shoe maker than Lev Tolstoy."

He smiled and retrieved from his drawer Babushka Sofiya's hand-written tag, fastened it back to one of the shoes and returned the pair to us.

*

"Can we go to Vishenki please?" Lena asked me that evening in the metro.

I was surprised by her request, unable to decide if she had said that merely to please me or if she was genuinely interested to find out more about my Babushka Sofiya. I explained to her that the trip to Vishenki would need some planning and that in the autumn of next year I would be happy to take her there. She looked pleased, which still didn't dispel my doubts about her motives. She is just a little girl, I thought, still too naïve to have learned the art of manipulation. She should be happy living her own life unhindered by the need to remember.

To remember demands commitment. It's an effort not to forget. We always invest something of ourselves in the things or people we don't want to let go. The things so remembered partake bits of our own emotional being, our soul. Without feelings, memories turn impotent, unable to withstand the onslaught of the present moment, which demands our full engagement. Maybe that is the reason why faces that were so dear to us once upon a time become so ruthlessly estranged.

The other day a woman with a bucket of unwashed potatoes came and sat on a seat opposite. I looked at her, turned my face away, distracted by a toddler who had started crying. At my stop I came out of the train and lingered for a while outside enjoying the soft light of the autumn evening. Only then did I hear a whisper in my mind telling me that the middle-aged woman with the bucket was Klava, a fellow student at the university, who had dropped out because of a horrible murder in the family. Her stepmother had been killed by her older brother in a drunken rage. She didn't say hello, the reason for which was obvious, but why didn't I say anything?

The word *Zabyt'* (to forget) is made of two parts—*za* and *byt'*; the part *byt'* signifies to be, to exist, whereas the prefix *za* means outside, behind or beyond the bounds. Thus when we say *Zabyt'* we seem to imply that we wish to move that thing, person or event beyond the bounds of our immediate present. We don't want them to die or disappear without a trace but we want to displace them into a nether world where life and living are of some other order.

The prefix za, however, also denotes, to be in support of, to stand for, or to fight for something or someone. Hence when we say *Zabyt'* we want to express our support for *byt'* or *byt'io* (existence), for life, for that which exists here and now. We forget because we want to live. We forget because we live in hope for a better life. It's this wretched hope that demands that we forget the unforgettable.

Is this the reason why Babushka Sofiya decided to forget so much? Was it really so deliberate? I am surprised that she didn't tell me anything of significance about my mother. About my father there was hardly a word; just his name and the place he was born and the city near where he might have died. Of her own husband there was even less and yet she remembered the last smile of Graf Tolstoy. She kept the Tolstoy shoes made most probably by her father, whose hand she was holding as she walked on the platform and the movie camera caught her from behind.

She left a brief note in her diary with a date, 16th May 1945, underneath. A week earlier she would have witnessed the Victory-Day parade in the Red Square. That year she had turned forty.

I was a mere six-month old baby then. A few months would pass and my mother would disappear forever, deported to the Magadan camps in Siberia.

Perhaps then, just to keep safe the memory of the unforgettable moment of her childhood, she scribbled the short note in her diary and wrote the date, twice underlined. Not a word about her unfortunate daughter, my mother, but a whole paragraph about Graf Tolstoy.

Was it a clever trick or just a gesture of her helplessness?

Maybe she was scared that the tragedies of her time would empty the joy she must have felt, witnessing the fleeting smile of an old sage in a house on the platform of a railway station.

Maybe she was.

The Electric Dress

Atsuko is surprised to see an email from an unknown sender in her inbox.
It has arrived from India. She clicks open the mail and reads:

*My name is Amrita. I live in Chandigarh, the capital of a state in
Northern India. I am twenty-eight years old. My father, he died ten
years ago, was a master carpenter and wood carver. Without him I
wouldn't have become an artist. I paint and sculpt but the material I
enjoy working with most is sound. I am learning to create landscapes
of sounds. This is because when I was three I suffered a severe throat
infection that resulted in a complete loss of voice. I haven't spoken an
audible word since then. I am used to this disability now and don't
begrudge my fate anymore because the loss has been compensated by
a valuable gift: an acute sensitivity to all types of musical and non-
musical sounds.*

*I am attaching with this message a short movie (three and a half
minutes long) of one of my recent works. Any media-player will be
able to play it on a computer. I know that it doesn't convey the whole
vitality of the work but it will give you some idea of my intention. It
will also reveal the way your own work has influenced me. By sending
it to you I want to acknowledge your presence in my life.*

*But I have one more request—I would very much like to visit you
and see you work. I assure you that I won't trouble you with questions
and will try to keep as far as possible out of your way. And then if I
am good and if you have time and inclination I would very much like
to go to the gallery in Tokyo and see you with your* Electric Dress.

Atsuko opens the attached file and plays it a number of times. It shows
a beautiful young woman riding a male tiger. The woman is dressed in a red
quilted bridal gown with hundreds of tiny mirrors stitched on it. Here and
there in between the mirrors hang bunches of tiny brass bells. The woman

sits still holding the reins, then kicks the tiger with her heels. It begins to move, at first slowly, then gathers itself and takes a few leaps. The woman on the tiger turns her head and Atsuko sees the face. "She must be Amrita she thinks. But why is she smiling? As the tiger leaps the bells jingle. In the mirrors Atsuko sees Amrita's face flash and fade, flash and fade. It is a strange light and sound show but Atsuko likes it. Something inside her stirs up, and she is unable to keep sitting in front of the computer.

In the afternoon Atsuko shows the email and the movie to Akira, her husband. He too is impressed and they both agree that they should invite the young Indian artist to visit them.

*

The next morning Akira asks Atsuko if she hasn't changed her mind. He is concerned about Atsuko's health. In the last few years she hasn't been well. The mildest of colds have been knocking her down. "Your lungs are weak," the doctors tell her. They want her to move to a place warm and dry, but they know that she won't leave. "How can I? I am over seventy now and to be honest I haven't any urge to prolong my life beyond what my failing body can grant me of its own will." Sometimes she does feel sad, pining for times when she was young and possessed the energy to do whatever came to her mind. Now it is too hard even to entertain new ideas. But they do come, less frequently, but whenever they drop in she welcomes them with open heart and mind.

The ideas don't seed in her mind, she often tells Akira, but right inside her body and, like the little birds in the bird-house that Akira erected on the large cedar in the back garden, they live inside her, making her feel pregnant, kicking and thumping, eager to come out with a scream.

"No, I haven't changed my mind," she tells Akira and together they decide to send Amrita an invitation. She dictates and Akira types and then, worried that their English isn't good, they resolve to send the draft to one of Akira's friend in Nara, who can read and write English. As they wait for his response Atsuko suggests that they should record a short movie-clip for Amrita. They decide that Atsuko will sit outside in the garden and read the words of the message and Akira will shoot the movie. Before emailing Amrita the reply, they play the short movie again and discover that Atsuko's voice is almost inaudible. "This doesn't look and sound good," they tell each other but because Atsuko is exhausted, Akira convinces her that Amrita won't be offended, and that they shouldn't try to repeat the experiment because who knows what could go wrong the next time. Atsuko is surprised. She knows how fussy Akira always is—a perfectionist of the worst kind. But she doesn't argue with him.

The following day, the email message, edited carefully by Akira's friend, and the attachment are sent to Amrita. Atsuko likes watching how swiftly the computer does these weird things. She waits for a few minutes to receive the notification that the message has been delivered successfully. She is relieved. Lately most of her messages have bounced back. She has needed Akira to help her fix the problem, but the problem is simple—she has begun to make silly mistakes, adding an unwanted comma or omitting a letter or two in the address.

They don't hear anything back from Amrita for a few weeks. They begin to think it wasn't such a good idea to invite the young Indian artist to stay with them. During the day they keep themselves busy doing this or that in and around the house but at night in bed they can't stop talking about Amrita and her imminent arrival. As usual Atsuko asks questions and Akira keeps his replies brief, almost monosyllabic. Where will she sleep? Is she a vegetarian? What will she do for a week? Who will take her to Tokyo? Won't the winter be too cold for her and the summer too hot? What if she gets bored? What if I get one of my dreadful attacks? Shouldn't we ask young Hiroshi to come and stay with us? Is the house too small? Should we ask her to stay in a hotel? She'll be upset, won't she?

*

The house isn't that small. It consists of two conjoined dwellings. A square house with a pitched roof is where the two live. To its left stands a solid brick house with a flat roof. The two are connected with a covered alleyway. The one with a flat roof houses their separate studios. Each studio has a large

67

window looking out to the valley beyond the road and the little lake. The hill-slope behind the house is overgrown with large cedars and maples. The patch in front of the house contains several cherry trees, but it isn't a proper garden. Atsuko doesn't like the imposed discipline of a proper garden, which is why she has refrained from interfering with nature's own will to grow. To the right hand side of the house they live in, stands a very tall cherry which blossoms each spring with abundance.

A stairway outside the flat roofed house reaches the roof fenced on four sides with a painted railing. There is a little storeroom on the flat roof. The roof is Atsuko's favourite place to sit and rest, not only in the spring or autumn but in the winter as well, although the wind can become intolerable. Standing on the roof she can look around for kilometres beyond the valley and terraced rice fields.

"She is a true Osaka girl," Akira never fails to remind her and others, and Akira is right. Osaka is in her blood. "I like this place," she tells everyone, "so quiet and peaceful," but she hasn't fallen in love with it. Akira chose the place and he was, as always, right. She needed a place like this to heal herself, to come to terms with her predicament, and she is glad that the little house has cured her of her ills, but she misses Osaka very much, especially her studio on the third floor of the building right next to the railway loop line. "I miss the noise," she hasn't stopped complaining, "the neon lights, the cars braking and starting, most of all the trains."

Akira realised how hard it was for her to get decent sleep at night during the first few years. So what did he do? He went to Osaka station with a tape recorder and taped the rattling noise of her favourite train. The first night he played it for her, she couldn't stop smiling. "Why does he love me so much?" She had thought then.

There were times when living with her wasn't so easy. He could have left her forever and no one would have blamed him but he isn't one of those who give up easily. He has persisted and he will persist into the future as well. "No it wasn't romance or love," she remembers him telling the director who was making a short documentary about her. "I just liked the way she painted, the way she raised the brush and her arm and used her hand and fingers."

"He is lying," Atsuko, who was sitting next to him, had thought.

He's in love with me, she had said to herself, the first time he called on her with an invitation to join his Group Zero. She was pleased to be asked and agreed at once. But she had hardly suspected that one day she would agree not just to marry him, but to live with him whole her life. Still it happened and she is glad that it has. I am lucky she reminds herself often. No, she adds soon after, he is lucky too.

*

Amrita arrives on the last weekend in August. Hiroshi meets her at the Nara railway station and drives her to the house. Atsuko would have preferred her to come in April when the cherry trees in her orchard were in blossom or in October when the autumn spreads its colours over the hills and terraces, but for some or the other reason, Amrita could only come then.

It has been raining for three days. "Stupid typhoons," she mumbles, unable to hide her displeasure. Akira laughs. He is accustomed to her whining and whingeing, and if she blames him for the typhoons it is only because she has to vent her anger. For a moment he thinks he should tell her the little newspaper item he read the other day, which reported how some Muslim clerics truly believe that earthquakes are caused by women who behave badly. He rightly changes his mind, still the absurdity of the idea brings a smile and he looks away, avoiding Atsuko's piercing glance. "Relax, my dear," he wants to tell her and hug her or hold her hand.

They open the door to greet Amrita and see a very pretty young woman, almost as tall as Atsuko. They bow, Amrita takes a step forward and the two hug. The beautiful smell of youth, Atsuko thinks. She is jealous which both pleases and annoys her. As they come in and sit down, and Akira and Hiroshi set up the tea, she notices how beautiful Amrita truly is—thick dark hair gathered in a pony tail, right in the middle of the forehead a bright red spot, the *bindi*; her mouth perfectly shaped, a little scar on the edge of her upper lip; a nose-stud with a little white pearl, placed at the right spot in the right nostril; the eyes unimaginably large with a soft warm glow, prone, as she would realise later, to look away.

Surely she isn't so quiet and timid, Atsuko thinks. At times people who don't know her well have held a similar misconception of her and she banishes the idea. To be an artist you have to be strong and very determined. She came to know that very early in her life, and she is confident that any hint of fragility which Amrita displays is just an aberration. A woman who imagines herself riding a tiger must have character. As they sip tea, she notices how Hiroshi can't keep his eyes off her. At night she'll mention this to Akira who will confirm that she is right, that it will be hard not be impressed by young Amrita. "Perhaps we should ask him to stay with us," she asks and Akira agrees, convinced that they need his presence to make Amrita feel comfortable.

Sitting at the table they slowly begin to find a way to communicate with each other. The immediate intermediary is the writing pad, which Amrita takes out as soon as she sits down at the table. A writing pad in an embroidered cover and its loyal companion—not pen but a pencil. They speak a mixture of Japanese and English. Hiroshi adds a word here and a word there and Amrita scribbles her replies. The three are impressed by her handwriting, neat and emphatic. This process is a blessing; it gives them time to think, feel and formulate their thoughts before speaking. One of them talks and the rest look. Amrita listens and writes and they wait to read her response.

After a day or so they get used to the noises Amrita emits from her mouth and throat. Harsh and illegible at first, they quickly learn to decipher the sounds of words intended to be uttered by her. Each successful transaction brings them closer and thereby encourages Amrita to speak more. When needed she uses hands not only to gesticulate but also to touch, and the ease and grace with which she accomplishes the task both surprises and pleases Atsuko.

Watching Amrita 'talk' with her hands, Atsuko begins to think about the sensuous nature of touch. Why in spite of loving Akira so intensely, the desire to touch each other eluded them both? Was the omission deliberate

70

or just an oversight caused by their being what they are?

They both know that fibre is Atsuko's favourite material. No, not only fibre but anything that can be wrapped, folded, shredded and strung. So why has the feeling of touch remained obscure to her? Why hasn't she ever thought about it before?

*

The next morning, after finishing breakfast, Amrita opens her suitcase and unwraps two packets. The first contains two L-shaped embroidered hangings. There is a handwritten note folded with them. Hiroshi reads and translates: *These hangings are for Akira. They are called* sankhia. *They come from villages in the deserts of Western India. The women make them to mark the arrival of the festive season. They are hung in the doorways to welcome gods, good fortune and friends.*

Akira and Hiroshi pick one each and stand up holding the two hangings. The sight is wonderful. Three stripes framed by embroidered borders; each stripe contains an alternating sequence of trees and animals, the most common of which is a camel with an occasional tiger or an elephant. The main fabric is of light, off-white colour and the figures are bright—red, yellow, apple green and black.

"I hope it warms your heart," Atsuko says to Akira and both Amrita and Atsuko smile.

The second packet contains two pieces. The first is simpler than the hangings but equally impressive. The colours are passive and restrained. The large sheet is white with a tinge of sky blue. Its embroidered border encloses a space painted with animals—fish, ducks and elephants. The outlines of animals are marked with coloured dots. A large lotus is placed right in the centre of the sheet.

The embroidered sheet is a present for Atsuko, Hiroshi translates Amrita's note. *The style is called* Kantha. *It is popular with women in the villages of Bengal, a state in eastern India. Unlike the desert in western India, this place is lush green and the rain never stops.*

"What about the second piece?" Atsuko asks.

71

"It's for Atsuko to paint," Hiroshi reads the note scribbled by Amrita.

The second piece is large as well, 2x5 meters. It is yellowish. Atsuko touches it. It feels rough like a canvas.

Atsuko begins to paint in the afternoon. The sheet is spread on the floor of her studio, stretched and pinned carefully to remove any kinks or folds. Akira leaves the two alone in the studio. Hiroshi too disappears promising to come back in the evening. The afternoon is cloudless, the sun shines; light falls from the window and from the skylight in the roof. Amrita sits on a cushion near the wall.

Atsuko's studio is clean, orderly and smells of paint and oil. The cans of paint are lined along one of the walls. There are brushes, pens, pencils and other strange instruments, one of which is a large wooden divider. Atsuko picks it up and walks to the centre of the sheet and draws a large circle. She moves back, puts away the instrument and picks a can of paint and then stops to select the right brush. The paint is a dark haematite red. She paints the circle, starting from the outer circumference and then fills it with smooth flowing strokes. Before drawing and painting other circles on the sheet, Atsuko stands still, watching.

Amrita looks. She is growing old, she thinks. She notices how the lean body of Atsuko has shrunk. Atsuko, humped, as if folded onto herself, sways. Then she takes a step forward, picks up another can and paints the next circle. The rest of the circles are painted swiftly. They are all in thick bright colours: yellow, blue and green. The next step is to join the circles with threads of paint. Amrita watches how Atsuko stands swaying, arms folded, staring for minutes to add just a tiny little streak. She is fascinated by her socks: brown with black dots and marvels at the way she walks without making any noise.

As promised she doesn't ask any questions. There is no need. She has come prepared, has read everything there is to read about Atsuko, the famous Gutai woman, and her obsession with lights, bulbs, circles and threads. She just watches.

For a week they follow the same routine. In the morning after breakfast they either take a walk together or Hiroshi takes her out to temples and gardens. In the afternoon she watches Atsuko paint. The evenings are spent talking and looking at various objects from Atsuko's collection. Most often it's Akira who speaks, with Hiroshi interjecting to explain this or that word. Most of his stories are about Atsuko and her weird but magical, to use his words, artwork. He tells them about the dress she made in 1956. "It wasn't a dress," Atsuko corrects him, "but a whole wardrobe." Akira agrees and tells them how for months Atsuko with only a rudimentary experience of a seamstress sewed layers upon layers of clothing, equipped with secret pockets, hems, sleeves and joins. When the dress was ready for the exhibition, she went to the gallery, walked into the room dressed in it and started undressing in front of the visitors. "She was young, beautiful and quite daring," Akira reminisces, "and I was scared that she might undress completely. What a scandal it would have caused." But Atsuko didn't go that far, she had never intended to discard everything. She just performed the act of undressing: the coat changing into a kimono and the kimono into a simple nightshirt.

As Akira recounts the performance, Atsuko who has gone out of the room, comes back with a large notebook and opens it to show Amrita. The notebook contains sketches, designs and flow diagrams, outlining the dress and the performance. So the act was meticulously planned, Amrita thinks, and Atsuko, as if she has heard the thought, explains that the spontaneity with which she performed was just an illusion. She had to train hard and rehearse every move, even if unexpected things did happen that forced her to improvise and find the best solution on the run.

*

Amrita isn't used to the silence which surrounds the house. No Indian ever would be, but once she begins to feel the subtle rhythms of the world in and outside the house her unease disappears. The urgency with which she had wanted to immerse herself in the task of watching Atsuko work dissipates. She feels liberated and happy. The first week flashes past. The second however is different, marred by two events that overshadow her life for a very long time.

One morning Atsuko announces that she will take Amrita to show her the textile treasures of the Shosoin. Akira looks at her to confirm if that's what she really means. He knows Atsuko hates travelling, especially by car, but it seems Atsuko has already planned everything.

They start soon after breakfast. The day is cloudy but it isn't raining. Hiroshi drives. They ask Amrita to take the seat in the front with Hiroshi, and Akira and Atsuko sit in the back. It hasn't escaped Amrita's attention that both Akira and especially Atsuko want her to be with Hiroshi. She also understands that it isn't only because he speaks English. That she has found him interesting, particularly because of his work on the architecture of ancient Japanese temples and monasteries, is no secret, but she is determined that she won't allow herself to go any further. She hasn't recovered from the 'foolish adventure', to use her words, with Jerome, the Jamaican photographer she met in Liverpool that had blinded her with desire and led to the neglect of her art. The affair didn't last. She knew it wouldn't but that didn't stop her from falling into the trap. She had resolved there and then that she would never again let herself be carried away so recklessly. She is pleased that she has kept her word and fortunately it has paid off. The gains have been enormous, and not only in relation to her art. She could have very easily turned bitter, hating the whole world, but the grief she felt ushered in a state of contemplation, and so becalmed and humbled she began to find new moments of pure joy. "Bitterness," her father used to say, "kills art, and there isn't anything more malignant than hate." She is glad that she has gotten rid off the affliction before it could have crippled her for life.

On the way they stop at the Nara Museum to pick up Ito Murakami, a curator friend of Atsuko. Ito is married to a cellist from Helsinki who plays with a chamber orchestra in Kyoto. "She is our Trojan Horse," Hiroshi remarks. The allusion becomes clear to Amrita when they reach Todaiji Temple. The Shosoin treasures are kept locked away from the public but an exhibition of selected pieces is held each year in October at the Nara Museum. This year Ito has been asked to curate a display of ancient Japanese musical instruments stored in the treasure house, and so she is allowed access to the treasures.

They stop outside the temple complex and walk. It begins to drizzle. The umbrellas are out. As they reach the repository, it starts to pour. They all rush to take shade under the eaves of the tiled roof, except Amrita, who stands and watches the rain fall. Drops the size of large chickpeas rattle the tiled roof. A gale bends the sheets of water. The rattle ceases for a moment and starts again. Lightning flashes followed by loud thunder. For a second she thinks of joining the rest of the party near the tiled roof but the child in her impels her to stay and watch. The red-brown cypress wood glistens, the water bounces off the white gravel on the ground and the smell of wood and grass is intoxicating. Only then, she notices Hiroshi standing by her side asking her to come undercover, and she relents.

As they begin to walk toward one of the new ferro-concrete buildings that house the treasures, the rain peters out. Inside the main building, two monks greet them. One of them is old and stooped, the other very young, almost a teenager. They guide them to the closet where Ito has been working for the last few weeks. They put on special gowns, slippers and gloves and the inspection begins. Ito shows them a red sandalwood lute called biwa. It has five strings. The soundboard is inlaid with mother-of-pearl. A figure of a musician riding on a camel is painted on it. A second maple-wood biwa has four strings and is decorated with a painting of four musicians on the back of a white elephant. Ito is aware that both Atsuko and Amrita are more interested in textile material. She brings out a yellowish silk twill patterned with an orange motif of trees and leashed lions. The two are more impressed, however, by a Kyo-ganoko shibori—a piece of silk painted with a broad pattern of hand-tied resist dots. The dots resemble the white spots on a fawn.

They spend a couple of hours in the closet, before Atsuko shows signs of exhaustion. Ito, who needs to finish her work, stays back. They sit near a pond to eat the small picnic lunch Akira has packed for them and enjoy brief moments of sunshine. A herd of deers, three adults and two fawns stroll past grazing.

Driving back Hiroshi decides to leave the main highway in favour of more picturesque but narrow roads. It is raining. Atsuko and Akira doze off. Amrita feels sleepy as well but forces herself to keep awake. They drive over a wooden bridge, follow a large lake to their left and come to a winding stretch of road running along the edge of a little hill. A blue Toyota overtakes them.

The young woman in the front passenger seat of the Toyota winds down the window and pushes her head out to look at them and wave. Hiroshi smiles awkwardly. "Look," he says to Amrita pointing at two spotted deers leaping across the road. The blue Toyota skids, slows down for a moment and speeds off. Hiroshi slams on his brakes to stop. That's when they see a fawn lying injured on the road. Two deers wait on the other side of the road, looking in their direction. They come out of the car. The hind leg of the fawn is smashed. There is blood from a wound in the back. Its eyes are shut. The little body convulses, emitting short bursts of cries. Hiroshi pulls a piece of rug from the boot of the car, and with some help from Amrita, lifts the little beast up and places it in a cardboard box. Atsuko is sitting on the wet grass in the rain. She doesn't want her umbrella anymore. "Leave me alone," she blurts but Akira continues to stand beside her waiting. After a few moments, Atsuko rises, opens the front door and sits down in the car. Hiroshi and Amrita get back inside the car too. They drive away leaving behind the two deers still looking in their direction. Amrita turns her head to look as one of the deer hops on to the road, stopping at the spot where the fawn lay injured.

They stop at a vet clinic. The verdict is clear. "It won't pull through," they are told and the fawn is put down. Atsuko insists that they take it back home and Akira acquiesces. They dig a hole near the large cherry tree and the fawn is buried. It is quite late in the evening but the rain has stopped. The sky is clear and a large half-moon rises as they go inside.

Atsuko walks into her bedroom and shuts the door behind her. She remains there for the next two days and nights. "She'll be alright," Akira assures Amrita and asks her to keep herself busy. Hiroshi offers to drive her to Nara for a few days but she refuses, opting to stay in the house and work in Atsuko's studio.

*

The absence of Atsuko opens other opportunities and although Amrita is worried about her, she decides to plan the concept of her new work called *The Landscape of Wind.* The two main elements of the landscape are a cherry tree and a little fawn resting under it. Not far from the tree stand two wooden poles with a wire stretched between them. Three plain cotton sheets hang on it secured by a pair of pegs. Each sheet has three rectangular slits cut in such a way that they can be turned like pages of a book bound on one side. A walking track runs parallel to the wire between the poles and takes a sharp turn to reach the cherry tree. The viewers are asked to follow the track and touch the wooden pole. As soon as they touch one of the poles, they begin to hear the wind blow and the sheets start flapping, the book-like slits open and shut and the wooden poles begin to squeak. A voice asks the viewers to turn and look at the cherry tree, immersed now in the light of a full moon. They see the fawn and walk up to it. As they kneel to touch it, the fawn disappears.

She makes notes in her book, sketches the spatial design and as she begins to think about the sheets, she sees Akira walk in to the studio. She enquires about Atsuko and is told that she is getting better and that he has a plan to facilitate her recovery. "Can I help?" She asks and Akira tells her that that's why he has come to talk to her.

The plan is simple. To recreate Atsuko's *Electric Dress.* "Won't that be wonderful?' He asks. "Absolutely," she writes on her pad with a smiling face underneath. Soon they get busy. Akira retrieves Atsuko's sketches and they go looking for bulbs, neon tubes, wires and switches. Some tubes are broken and Hiroshi is phoned to come in and help. He is sent away to shop for bulbs and wires. When he returns they discover that the switchboard with the timer needs replacement. He agrees to make a second trip and Amrita decides to go with him. On the way Hiroshi tells her the story of the famous bench on the Osaka railway station. Amrita pleads with him to take her there. "Not today," he says, "but when I drive you to the Kansai International Airport." "Wonderful," she wants to say and plants a little kiss on his cheek.

Akira and Amrita work on the dress. By Monday night the dress is almost finished. The only thing that remains to be done is to test it and to see if it can be safely put on. Akira wants Amrita to try it on but because they both are tired they put it off till the next morning.

The following morning Atsuko is at the breakfast table. She looks pale and tired but the smile on her face suggests that she is ready to talk and listen. She asks for Hiroshi, and Akira informs her that Hiroshi has gone to his studio in Nara to prepare a lecture for a conference, and that he will return in the evening to join them for a farewell dinner. Atsuko appears confused and Akira tells her that Amrita is flying back tomorrow. Atsuko gets off her chair and asks Amrita to follow her into her studio.

"I have something to show you," she tells her. In the studio, Atsuko requests Amrita to help her open an old wooden chest. It contains an assortment of odd objects and a set of notebooks, clothbound and neatly tied by coloured ribbons. Atsuko opens one of them, locates the right page and smiles. 14 August 1956, Amrita reads the date and underneath sees the sketch of an electric circuit with a bell. "Do you know about my bells?" she asks Amrita, who nods yes, and Atsuko retrieves a little doorbell from the chest. The purple enamel has peeled off, but it feels wonderful to touch.

"This is for you," Atsuko hands Amrita the bell, "to make sounds." *Arigato gozaimasu (Thank you)*, Amrita shows her the Japanese characters she had asked Hiroshi to scribble in her notebook.

They spend most of the afternoon on the roof above the studio. The day is warm, illumed by a bright sun. The breeze is soft and wafts around them like a thin sheet of silk. The water in the distant lake glistens. An old man is sitting with a fishing rod. A little girl in a dark blue parka skips behind him. She drops the rope, runs to the old man and embraces him. The old man gets up. The little toddler is sitting on his shoulders. Atsuko laughs a giggly girlish laughter and suddenly begins to talk about her artist father and her peaceful but lonely childhood in Osaka. She didn't have any siblings and her mother, a strict disciplinarian, didn't want to spoil her for that reason. Her father on the other hand treated her like a princess. "You don't have a child of your own?" Amrita wants to ask but doesn't know the right way to say it.

*

Hiroshi comes well prepared for the dinner. A bottle of nice Australian wine and a framed object wrapped in paper. He gives the present to Amrita and bows. The present is unwrapped. It is a large coloured print of a photo. There is Amrita standing in the middle of the photo holding her umbrella. The sheet of rain hangs in the air pierced sharply by a bright streak of lightning; behind her stands a large maple which glows like a large Japanese lantern.

The dinner is relaxed, the conversation easy and the atmosphere warm but melancholic. Atsuko appears at peace with herself and although she hasn't returned to her whimsical and talkative best, the signs are there that she will soon rediscover her lost form. Akira however is tense. During the dinner they drop hints about the *Electric Dress* just to see how Atsuko will react to the version they have managed to recreate. They don't want to shock her in any way.

After the dinner is finished Akira and Hiroshi wheel in the dress. It rests on a small wooden platform with a metal rod in the middle. Atsuko doesn't react, just looks for a moment, gets up, walks up to it, adjusts a few bulbs and wires and inserts the plug. She turns in their direction and clicks on the switch. Nothing happens for a moment. She takes out the plug, examines it and the timer, adjusts the timer, inserts the plug and presses the switch. The dress lights up, flooding the room with flashing lights. Suddenly one of the red neon lights blows off. Akira replaces it.

The time has come to ask the important question: does she want to try it on? They wait and wait. All of a sudden, Atsuko tells Amrita to get up and put on the dress. Amrita looks in the direction of Akira not knowing what to do. When Atsuko repeats her order, the firmness in her voice can't be ignored. Atsuko watches as Akira and Hiroshi remove the dress from the platform and help Amrita to put it on. Once the dress is on, all the connections and wires are checked again and again and the switch is turned on.

Amrita stands still for a moment and then noticing a large friendly smile on Atsuko's face takes a few steps to the left, then to the right, and after gaining confidence does a slow pirouette. "Just like me," they hear Atsuko exclaim, and she claps. Akira and Hiroshi join in.

"Look, look …" they suddenly hear Hiroshi's voice and turn in the direction of the television. During the dinner, Akira had turned it on to watch the Paris recording of Stravinsky's *Firebird*. The sound had been switched off just before they started playing with Atsuko's *Electric Dress*.

What they see now on the television is unworldly. A large jet airliner flies in the direction of a tall tower and crashes into it, followed by another that crashes into the second tower of glass and concrete and the two crumble. The camera shows people running, shouting, screaming. There is dust in the sky lit up by a fire as they see people jumping from the windows.

The report of the newsreaders at the desk explains the scene: It's New York. The time is 8.50 am (9.50 pm in Tokyo) and the date 11 September 2001.

Amrita wants to sit down but can't because of the dress. She stands watching the shots of the crumbling twin towers overlayed by the flickering neon lights of the *Electric Dress*.

After a few moments Akira switches off the television, and he and Hiroshi help Amrita take off the dress. It is hung back on the wooden platform and wheeled out.

No one says a word. They sit together in silence. Atsuko is the first to get up. She walks off into her bedroom followed by Akira. Hiroshi stays in the room. He will sleep the night in the house.

Amrita goes into her room to pack for her flight home the next day.

"Good night," Hiroshi says. Amrita smiles.

Silence reigns in the house. Outside there are only whispers.

*

The next day Amrita departs. They say goodbye promising to meet again. Hiroshi drives her to the airport and as promised he takes her to the bench on the platform of the Osaka station where many years earlier Atsuko had come to sit down. He repeats the story told by Atsuko "There is a bench on the platform where she often used to sit waiting for the train. That evening she was late and feeling tired. She decided to rest on the bench before walking home. She looked around and saw on the tall buildings outside, neon signs advertising cough syrups and pain killers. She liked the sight. That's when she said to herself that she would make a dress of neon lights and go to a gallery and dance like beautiful Ophelia. That's it. Simple."

On the way to the airport they listen to the news on the radio and try to comprehend the enormity of what they witnessed on the television the night before. They hear people talk about the event endlessly, with grief, anger, and uncontrollable rage. Among many other words spoken on the radio that day they hear words such as Hiroshima and Nagasaki. The presence of these words makes them uneasy, any attempts to ignore these names only makes their presence even more real, but they keep quiet, knowing that no conversation can help them understand the absurdity of human life.

At the airport they hug each other and kiss.

*

In time Amrita receives from Atsuko the unfinished painting she had started to paint for her. The accompanying brief note explains everything: "Sorry, can't paint any more. There is no point. I feel old and useless. Unfinished, it looks better. Don't you think?"

She hangs the unfinished painting alongside Hiroshi's framed coloured print. In time a series of postcards gather around it. They include photos of Hiroshi's wife Keiko and their son Akira; a picture-postcard showing Moscow's Red Square, and a photo of Atsuko on the Charles Bridge in Prague. A year later Amrita meets Hiroshi, Keiko and the young Akira and accompanies them to Lumbini, the birth place of the Buddha.

Life goes on and the detritus of each day drops into the memory but among the debris one moment shines like white flint—Atsuko adjusting the *Electric Dress* over Amrita's head. Its presence is real, almost physical and each time she sees herself in the dress, she lowers her head as if trying to help Atsuko. But what surprises Amrita most is her inability to translate this precise moment into her art. She tries to compel herself to do something with it, but after a few torturous attempts she gives up, leaving the moment alone, untouched, unsoiled. Her submission brings rewards—the moment, like a benevolent Ganesha, comes to reside with her, invisible but real, removing with his smile all hurdles, opening new doors and walking with her.

For more than a decade she keeps returning to the motifs of the cherry tree and the fawn in her artwork, one of the most striking of which is a self-organising sculptural installation visualised on a large digital screen. The viewers in the gallery are asked to make a whistling noise and a heap of bones, tissues, flesh and skin turn into a spotted fawn that disintegrates after a few minutes. Moments of appearance and disappearance become the true signature of her future artworks.

But there in one blind spot in her memory that disturbs her. She can recall the crumbling towers she saw on the television. She can also recall how the lights from the *Electric Dress* she wore that night flickered and flashed, but she can't remember the emotions she felt watching the incident. Perhaps that is why the crumbling towers haven't found a place in her artwork. Her friends sometimes ask her why, but she doesn't answer. Her silence confuses them even more, and if she is pressed hard, she just says: "I don't know. I am not ready yet."

She is puzzled that the savage brutality of the event didn't move her but she resists the temptation to find a valid explanation.

Dance is Like Water

As I stepped out of the Joyce Theatre that late evening in March, I suddenly remembered my father's little house located on one of the busiest streets in Madras. It was indeed his house; we—my mother, my four younger sisters and I—knew that very well. No one had ever said so explicitly but there was never any doubt that he was the master, ruling the house and our lives. Sarla, the oldest of my sisters, used to call him a benevolent tyrant but he was a tyrant first and foremost. The benevolence which he sometimes showed us, especially to Sarla, I am more than certain now, was both calculated and targetted. Nothing was ever done without a purpose. Like all despots he was shrewd and unforgiving.

Perhaps that is why I was surprised that I suddenly remembered the house. Why now? Why here? I asked, trying to drive the image away, but it lingered and I gave up, hoping that it would fade.

I left Madras in 1971, and since then I haven't set foot in India. The last letter I wrote to Sarla was in December 1972. Her little note with a photo is still with me, tucked inside one of the drawers of my desk.

Once, fleetingly, I thought I saw Jessica in the theatre. It was definitely her. Older and a little plump. She must have given up dancing, I thought, as I watched her turn and wave from the third row. I didn't know whether to wave back. Then the lights dimmed. Good, I said to myself. Now it would be easy to slip out unnoticed. "How is Lara?" I am sure that is the question she would have asked, and I didn't have the slightest desire to talk to anyone about Lara.

I walked out of the theatre, returned to my hotel, spent the night fast asleep in my room and took the early morning flight back to my little house in Menlo Park in California.

*

My name is Visnu K Mahalingam. They call me VML. I don't know how and when the letter K was dropped from my name. My friends at the university must have decided that it was spurious and, like a vestigial appendix, had to undergo verbal surgery. Only Lara gave the letter proper recognition, although she knew that it stood for my father's name. Coming from her it didn't sound out of place and I accepted it, like I accepted everything that Lara said and did. Lara was like that. You had to take her as she was, fully or not at all.

Lara's father, Valery Grossman, was a Russian Jew and her mother, Vincenta Mendoza, a devout Catholic, who had, so she thought, found the right balance between God and Marx; a balance adopted, with minor modifications, by Lara too. I suppose that is why it didn't come as a surprise when one day out of the blue Lara asked me if I wanted to travel with her to Santiago; not to meet her parents but to play with her little dance troupe. "Of course," I said. Luckily, she didn't ask me why. "Because I loved her," wouldn't have satisfied her, and to say that I believed in everything she did wouldn't have been right either.

I met her on September 18, 1971. It was a Monday and the time: seven past five in the evening. I remember the exact minute, not because I wrote it down in my diary but because I haven't forgotten even the tiniest detail about that moment.

That evening we didn't talk but I knew that we would come to that soon.

A week earlier I had bought a South Indian *mridangam* in an antique shop on Third Avenue, between 25th and 26th street. I was walking past the shop and in the shop window I saw a few musical instruments, one of which was the *mridangam*. It was quite expensive and yet I bought it because it was very similar to the one I used to play at home. The middle-aged woman who sold me the instrument didn't know much about it and I didn't want to divulge any more information, scared that she would ask me to pay more. She wanted me to play but I declined, rushed with the instrument back to my room and tried it out. It needed tuning and I cursed myself for not asking the woman if she had tuning accessories for it. The next morning the shop was shut. The notice on the door said that Mary, the woman at the shop, had gone away to attend a funeral and wouldn't be back for a week.

So on September 18, I walked up to the shop again and discovered that Mary had fallen ill and I had to explain to the young man standing in for her the reason I had returned to the shop. He listened to me without showing any apparent interest, walked into a store cupboard at the back of the shop and came out with a wooden box. The box contained a wooden block and a little slab of stone. It also contained a set of *manjiras*. I bought them as well, and the young man gave me the wooden block and the slab for free. "Enjoy," he said.

As I stepped out of the shop, it began to rain, light but cold. I walked, shielding my head with my backpack. Luckily it soon stopped and by the time I reached 32nd street I was dry. Just near a garbage bin I saw a dead pigeon and a young boy poking it with a stick. I stopped waiting for the boy to leave the bird alone, and that was when I heard the sound of drums. I looked around, located the general direction of the sound, crossed the street and discovered that it was coming from a room on the third floor of a building. I found the stairs and walked up. The door was open and I didn't know if I should go in. Then I saw a woman sitting on the floor. She looked at me, smiled and waved for me to come in. I went in and sat next to her. The woman was Lara, or Larissa Grossman, as she introduced herself to me formally a week later.

*

A few months after my tenth birthday, my father ruled that I should give up any thought of going to college. The explanation was simple: "You are my eldest son, and it's your duty to look after the school."That was it. He made it clear that he expected me to learn everything about Bharatanatyam: the songs, the music and the basic principles of *rasa-shastra*. When I mentioned to him that Sarla, who was more interested in dancing than me, and who wanted to learn and teach, would do a better job, I was told to shut up. So I shut up, and, just to satisfy him, learnt whatever he taught me. However, I still managed to study at the college and finish the degree with high grades and a score of medals.

Mr White, the principal of St. John's School, played an important role in deciding my fate. One day he came to our house wanting to talk to my father. From him my father learnt that I had a special, almost instinctive, feel for mathematics and that if nurtured properly I could turn out to be as brilliant as Mr Ramanujan, the famous Indian mathematician. He listened to him patiently and thanked him for being kind to his son and respectful to him and his family, but said that the question was settled and that it was obligatory for him to make a dance-guru out of me.

Fortunately Mr White didn't give up on me and helped me as best as he could. He arranged special after-hours tuition and convinced the authorities to grant me exemption from compulsory military training in the NCC, the National Cadet Corp. In order to keep me healthy and fit, the Society of Jesus that ran the school arranged special food rations for me and my family.

However, to suggest that I wasn't tempted by dance and music isn't correct. It was impossible not to be tempted. My father ran a small but successful dance school at home, recommended highly by none other than Rukmini Devi who visited our house seeking my father's advice. Her name and contacts helped him to enrol students from all over the world.

I especially remember a woman by the name of Georgie Joyce who arrived one day from Melbourne and stayed with us for more than a year. That year I graduated with honours from my college. Mr White came to attend the awards ceremony instead of my father, who although proud of my achievement, and this I came to know from Sarla many years later, declined to acknowledge it in any shape or form because of his pride and also out of shame that I had ignored his wishes and undermined his authority.

Georgie was a few years older than me, and although my father had arranged for her to stay in a separate room in a block across the street from us, she chose to live with us, which I am certain wouldn't have been easy. No shower, no toilet bowl and paper and no washbasin. Like us, she used to sit on the floor to eat and sleep on a *dhari*, next to Sarla.

I have to thank Georgie for helping me to decide my future. She read the letter that Mr White had received from the dean of Columbia University offering me a scholarship at the graduate school. She asked me about my research and I told her about my interest in topology and in the theory of knots and strings.

"Do you really want to go?" she asked.

"Absolutely," I replied.

"Then go," she said. She told me not to worry about my father, who, she was sure, had no choice other than to reconcile himself to what I did. "Look," she said, "if I can come to Madras against the wishes of my mother, you can do it as well. Just pack up and go."

"But you are English," I said, "free and independent."

"No, not English, Irish," she replied and gave me two addresses. One in Melbourne and the other that of her aunt in New York. "Write to me, when you are there. I might come and visit you," she said.

Before leaving I did ask my father to forgive me for disobeying him, hoping that he would at least soften his stance, but unfortunately he didn't. "Now that you have decided to go," he said, "don't come back. Never. I don't want to see you again."

*

After our first few meetings I realised that Lara wasn't interested in my work at the university. However, this didn't worry me, and whenever I had time I went with Lara to watch her train with Merce Cunningham's small company. The company didn't need new dancers but many young artists like Lara were allowed to watch, learn, and whenever possible, join the class.

I liked watching Merce teach and rehearse. He never spoke much at all, but whenever he felt the need the phrases were often interrupted by short bursts of laughter. His voice had a rather soft, whispering quality, which always made me think that he wasn't quite sure of what he was saying or going to say. But this was an illusion. He wasn't a very tall man: just five feet eight or ten. Rather slim but strong without a skerrick of fat. Brownish eyes set deep, thick eyebrows, short wispy hair, his receding hairline exposing a large forehead, long sharp nose, thin lips and a face scribbled with wrinkles. He usually sat on a wooden chair with a tall stool at his side. On the stool: a notebook, pen and a stopwatch. He sat with his hands resting on his thighs, his neck stretched out like that of an egret, eyes looking sharply.

Even as he sat there, one could see that he was wound up like a spring ready to uncoil at any moment. When it came, the moment was utterly magical. I have never seen anyone so wonderfully animal-like: the sheer agility, the ability to turn unexpectedly, to leap high and float in the air as if he had wings and then land with immaculate ease, precision and grace.

"You are lucky," Lara said to me when I told her that Merce had once allowed me to watch him rehearse the very first movements of his new composition. She assumed that it was because of my mridangam. She was only partly right. I remember Merce asking me about the research I was doing at the university. I explained to him, very briefly, the hyperbolic theory of knots, that by tabulating various types of knots mathematicians hoped to understand the shape of space around us. He didn't quite believe me when I told him that they had already described more than six billion knots. "Show me a few," he asked, and I drew in his notebook the shapes and notations of primary knots tabulated by Alexander and Briggs. "How fascinating," he said and showed me sketches of movements he had choreographed for *Summerspace*. The apparent similarity between the two was striking. He rose from his chair and began to dance the movements. That day we talked about computers, punching cards and FORTRAN language. I told him that in the not too distant future it would be possible to program and store various movement-phrases of his dances on a computer.

"Not only store," he mused, "but invent new movements as well." He was right because once the first few phrases of a shape have been defined and coded, the computer can create a series of viable and non-viable movements.

But what about the *mridangam*? Did it also play some role in helping me find a place in Merce's studio? Most definitely. It happened on the fateful evening of my first meeting with Lara. I sat with her for a couple of hours watching the group rehearse. I also saw Lara join the class and dance. Tired, I decided to go. I picked up my backpack and, as I got up, the stone slab, the wooden block and the *manjiras* fell out. Luckily the group had already stopped dancing. I told them that back home in India I played the mridangam and that the two weird objects, the slab and the wooden block, were used to tune the instrument. There was a woman in the studio who had played in John Cage's percussion ensemble. She asked me to bring the mridangam next time and play for them.

*

Lara's uncle, the elder brother of her step-father, had a small beach house near Wildwood, a few kilometres north of Cape May. Lara invited me to stay at the house for a few months in the summer break of 1972. We were not alone. Iris, a young woman from Toronto, and Philippe, an Italian from Chicago, had also come. The three of them had been training together for a while.

The house was a few minutes' walk from the beach. The town itself was rather small and unfriendly and yet it was a welcome escape from the giant metropolis which induced a sense of awe and fear in me. I felt oppressed by its size, squashed by the buildings towering over me like alien monsters in a sci-fi movie, their bright lights outshining the night sky. I was scared that soon I'd forget the shape and look of a starlit sky. The streets, the bridges and even the statue of Liberty made me appear small, insignificant, inconsequential.

That summer Lara's small troupe had planned to choreograph and rehearse a few short compositions which they were hoping to perform in the city. Lara never called herself a dancer. "I am a performance artist," she would proudly declare. One of her friends had once shown her a video of a performance by Atsuko Tanaka, a Japanese Gutai artist, and had decided that she would like to do something similar. She took Merce's classes to free her body of the contrived movements she had learnt as a child in a ballet school in Santiago. She found the narrative, the music and the choreography of classical ballet unnatural, contrary to the organic impulses of human bodies. Merce's dancing freed the body, revealing how bodies shape the same movement differently. Lara's profound dislike of ballet was overstated, I know. But it did make me aware of the way my father used to instil discipline in his dancers, forcing them to follow him without ever questioning his judgement. He had the backing of his religion, its sacred texts and tradition, and the authority he commanded over his students was expressed in one simple word: *guru*. That is what he was, and the daily ritual of bowing to him and touching his feet reinforced his position of authority.

Lara liked to rehearse Merce's exercises and dances again and again. Her favourite was *How to Pass, Kick, Fall and Run*. "I go to Merce to unlearn," she used to say, "to cleanse my body of the detritus so that it is ready."

Ready for what? I wanted to ask. That she was getting her body ready for the magic to happen became clear to me at the beach house. Most of the day the three of them rehearsed, learning from each other. I played the *mridangam* whenever I was asked, all the time hoping that they wouldn't force me to perform some moves of my father's Bharatanatyam. Luckily they didn't.

One night before going to bed Lara asked me if I was enjoying Neruda. She had recently bought me a bilingual edition of his selected poems. I read to her *Solo la Muerte*. "I like it too," she said, "especially the first stanza with its *oscuro, oscuro, oscuro*." To be honest her *oscuro, oscuro, oscuro* sounded far more emphatic than the English *dark, dark, dark*. I asked her to read me some more and she obliged, reading several poems from *Residencia en la Tierra*. That night I saw her in my dream, walking on the beach either pregnant or holding the hand of a little boy. The boy, just two or three years old, released her hand and ran towards the water. "Pablo," I heard her call. Once, twice, and she ran. Her hat blew off in the wind and then the two of them, she and her Pablo, disappeared.

I never got the chance to tell her about the dream at the beach house because I found her busy with more important things. For more than a week she and her friends worked on various moves, shapes and structures.

I watched them amazed by how different the three of them looked, especially Philippe. His body worked in spasms and bursts which seemed to emphasise the flow and continuity of what Lara and Iris did. Iris was taller than Lara, much straighter, and erect, and her short hair and long ears complemented the shorter, more curvaceous, muscular and angry-looking Lara. If Lara had a tendency to leap and fly, Iris preferred the solid ground beneath her feet.

That day Lara recorded seven of Neruda's poems, which included three or four of those she had read to me the night before. The first in the sequence was *Solo la Muerte*. She played the tape as they danced. I was asked to improvise on the mridangam. I soon noticed that the magic for which she had trained her body was beginning to happen. The moves, the words and the sound of my mridangam were coming together.

It took four to six weeks to remove the kinks and by the end of July the dance-cycle was ready to be performed at a number of street venues. However, for the final version of the cycle she used the recording in the voice of Valery, her father. He must have done the recording on a beach because you could hear the waves in the background. The tape with his recording came with a note in which he warned Lara to stay away from Santiago. "It isn't safe here," he warned not knowing that his warning was like a red rag to Lara.

"I want to go," she said. "Do you want to come?"

"Of course," I replied.

*

A few weeks after I returned from New York, I found the tape, not the one in Valery's voice but the first one, the working version in which Lara read five of the poems in Spanish.

With the tape I also found a few other things which I had completely lost track of. One of them was a packet from Georgie. After returning from India, Georgie lived for a few years in Dublin with her grandmother and then returned to Melbourne where she and a dancer from Bali opened a school of Indian classical dance and music.

Once, on my way back from New Zealand, I stopped for a few days in Melbourne. Georgie took me to the school and introduced me to her Balinese friend and to some of their talented students. One of them asked me to play the *mridangam* and I couldn't say no. I am glad that I was asked because after returning from Santiago I had decided to ignore the instrument completely. I was no doubt rusty and my first few attempts lacked confidence but it took only ten minutes or so to rediscover the skill I had willingly set aside.

Georgie also told me about Sarla who taught music and dance in a university in Auckland. She wanted to give me her address and phone number but I told her that I wouldn't need them. From Georgie I found out that my mother had died a couple of years after I left India and that my father was still alive, old, and frustrated, but healthy. Georgie told me that my father's dance school ceased to exist ten years ago and that my father now lived on the money sent to him by his three daughters, two of whom had moved to Dubai with their husbands.

"You are still on your own?" I remember her asking me.

"It's easy that way," I must have replied.

"You haven't got over Lara?" was her next question and although I was annoyed by her tone I didn't say anything because Georgie is a friend and friends should be allowed to speak their mind. I didn't want to know how and from whom she could have heard about Lara. My lack of response must have convinced her to drop the subject.

I run a small software company that writes computer programs for a few well-known multinationals selling computer games and other similar simulation packages. The job is easy and doesn't require much intellectual effort. The knots and strings which used to interest me a lot as well have been forgotten. I have lost all interest in any form of art and I tend to avoid reading anything other than crime novels.

I am drifting, I often say to myself, towards that moment after which I'll cease to exist. Forgetting will happen only then. I live because I have to, and each moment that I live is shared with Lara. She is always with me and in me and I don't want it to be any other way.

My Spanish has improved and once a year when Valery visits me, we talk only in Spanish. Each time we say goodbye he doesn't forget to remind me that this will be his last visit. "I am getting old you know," he says and laughs.

*

Valery met us at the airport in Valparaiso and although he said that he was happy to see us, it was clear that he hadn't wanted us to come. Lara's mother had already left Santiago, unable to endure the upheavals. She and her husband, a Cuban, were living in Florida.

We stayed in Valparaiso for a week during which Lara gathered her small troupe, called *Faro*, which included Victor, the guitarist, and Isabella, who used to train with Lara at the ballet school. Lara's intention was to tour mining villages, farms and factories and to perform for the "poor". We travelled in crowded trains and buses and often hitchhiked with tourists from Europe, Australia and Canada.

The program we performed was simple and didn't change significantly. We often started with a piece which we thought would cheer the audience up. It was an improvisation after one of Merce's famous dances, the one in which the dancer struggles to put on a jumper with no neck opening. Often I acted out the dance, accompanied by Victor on the guitar. This was followed by three or four pieces from the dance-cycle based on Neruda's poems. The dance cycle was called *Explico algunas Cosas* (*I'm Explaining a Few Things*), which was the title of one of the poems. Often we played a recording of the poems. In one mining village we met a young poet who wished to read the poems himself. His name was Raphael. He wanted to tour with us but had to change his mind because his mother had fallen ill.

In a little fishing village we performed in front of a small church. The crowd was rather small: five old women and a man on crutches. After the second dance, the priest from the church came out and asked us to leave and we left. The women protested but the priest didn't relent. Unfortunately, or perhaps fortunately, we were forced to stop our performances quite a few times.

We were arrested eventually in Rancagua, two weeks after Allende's suicide on September 11, 1973. Lara had been looking forward to it. She was burning with rage and ready to throw herself to the wolves in uniforms. "Cowards," she called them. After the events of September 11, I had suggested that we should keep low for some time and tone down our performances by erasing some lines from the poems, such as *Generales, Traidores: Mirad mi casa muerta* (*Treacherous Generals: see my dead house*). I told her that it wasn't wise to end the performances with the words: *Venid a ver la sangre por las calles* (*Come and see the blood in the street*). But Lara wouldn't listen, and I didn't want her to tell me to "run away and hide" as she had told Victor and Isabella, who had found reasons to leave the troupe.

Because we were arrested by the army guards and not the police, I knew it wasn't going to end well. We were about to begin the performance in the street, which, if I remember correctly, was called Independencia. The city of Rancagua is located around forty kilometres east of the El Teniente Copper Mine. That is why most of the population was in some way or other associated with the mine and the company, which also sponsored the main football club in the city. A large river, the Rio Cachapoal, runs to its south. I remember the river well, because of the night I had spent sheltering under the bridge.

After our arrest we were taken to the barracks just a few hundred metres from the bridge. I wasn't interrogated. One of the soldiers punched my face hard, kicked me a few times and ordered me to leave. But how could I have left Lara alone in the barracks? I sat outside for a few hours, then crossed the bridge and saw an old man sitting near a camp fire. He looked at my bruised face, smiled and offered me a bowl of potato and corn soup. We didn't talk. After finishing his soup he got into his sleeping bag and sat leaning against the damp concrete pillar. I offered him a cigarette, which he refused, and then he went to sleep.

In the morning I phoned Valery who arrived that evening. He came with a list of the names of important officers who he thought might be of some help. The list helped. After three days we were told that Lara had been transferred to an army barrack in Santiago. In Santiago one of

Valery's acquaintances found out that Lara had been handed over to the police and that we should go to the central prison. We waited for two days to get some news about her.

By then Vincenta had joined us as well. She looked terrible. She was angry with me for not looking after Lara and for leaving her alone in the barracks.

The waiting ended that Friday afternoon when a friend drove the three of us to the central prison and told us to wait for him. After an hour and a half he emerged with a woman guard. She wanted one of us to go inside with her to identify the body. Vincenta declined. Valery and I went inside.

Lara was cremated the next day in Valparaiso and her ashes were scattered over the sea.

*

A few years ago Valery, on one of his annual visits, showed me a photocopy of the post-mortem report he had managed to obtain with the help of one of his friends in the army. One short paragraph of the report was marked by an orange highlighter. I only read the highlighted part. Valery wanted me to keep the report. I declined. That Lara was eight weeks' pregnant didn't surprise me. I knew that. And it didn't surprise me at all that I could read the report without showing any signs of distress, anger or sadness. However, for a very brief moment, the thought came to me that I should tell him the dream I had had at the beach house in Wildwood many years ago. I looked at his sad face and decided against it.

Instead we watched a tape of Merce's *Winterbranch*. I don't know why but somehow the tape happened to be in the video player and I clicked it on. The tape began to play and as soon as I heard La Monte Young's *Two Sounds*, I remembered in a flash that I have lived with these two sounds forever. That Lara and the sounds are inseparable. That the ways of falling she had learnt from Merce, and rehearsed, aren't soundless movements of a body devoid of emotions. That if I have stopped grieving it isn't because I have stopped feeling sad but because the sounds have kept the grief alive but bearable.

"Dance is like water," Merce often said, "because like water it seeps through your fingers." I am sorry, Merce, this isn't quite true. It is elusive only when we want to describe it in words. Otherwise it is solid and tangible. Like bodies it makes you feel hurt, grief and joy. It touches you, like Lara still does and always will.

But all that is solid melts into air: Lara used to quote her Marx in Spanish. It went like this: *Todo lo que se creía permanente y perenne se esfuma.* As I speak these words I feel Lara in my mouth, the whole of her, like the roughened seed of a plum. I keep the taste alive, doing my best not to swallow the seed. I won't let it melt into air. Never.

The Dreams of Johann Ulrich Voss

"Stop it," she scolds herself, but stop she can't. Tears roll and her body shakes for a few moments after which the crying changes into sobs. That's when she, as if under a strange spell, imagines herself looking at her close-up beamed on the screen of a cinema and begins to smile.

"A boy in a girl's body," that's what her Dad used to say about her. "Not at all," her Mama would object, but in her heart she knew that her Maya wasn't an ordinary girl. Her Mama was right. No pain, hurt or offence was strong enough to make her cry. This troubled her Mama because she didn't want Maya to turn out like her—dry, detached and heartless. She wanted her to inherit a bit of her Dad's cuddly softness, making her more accessible. Harry, Maya's Dad, was a softy, who didn't need any special reason to break into tears. Like tears, smiles and laughter came easily to him. It didn't matter if he was crying or laughing, his whole body gave itself to the act fully.

She opens her bag, pulls out a packet of tissues and wipes her face and notices a little woman in a large hat standing in front of her holding a bouquet of carnations. The woman says something to her and wants to touch and pat her. Maya doesn't understand the words but assumes the old woman is trying to find out if she is alright. "I'm OK," she blurts and the woman slowly walks away from her, leaving her alone on the bench in the park.

*

This is her third day in Budapest. She flew to Vienna from Sydney, spent a day there, then caught the train and arrived in Budapest late evening on Sunday. Tired from being squashed in an economy class seat, she spent the whole of Monday and most of Tuesday sleeping in her small apartment. The few hours she was awake were surrendered to her soul-mate, the Apple notebook, surfing on the web, checking her mail, listening to music or watching her favourite *As Time Goes By* on the BBC's iPlayer. The inbox overflowed with messages from Dad, asking her if she was okay. She replied to all of them with: "Don't worry Dad. I am fine. Haven't been mugged, raped or lost. Love you." She added the obligatory but not formal signs: X, ☺ .

There was a brief message from Andrew. He was upset with her for not telling him she was flying overseas. He'll survive, she thought. "I am nasty, aren't I?" She thought and the thought to her great surprise, brought her even more satisfaction.

She considers herself to be a well-organised traveller who plans everything before leaving. On this trip she has brought a series of maps, the largest of which is a street map of Budapest, printed on an A0-size sheet, on which she has marked in red crosses the places she intends to visit. There is a circled cross near the intersection of Dosza-Gyorgy Utca, running almost north-south, and a smaller street named Dembinszky Utca. At that site she hopes to find an apartment in a five-storeyed block. This is the apartment she has come to see and, if she is fortunate, to spend a night there. The other, equally important place she wants to visit is a smallish building not far from the Orthodox Synagogue. It houses a high school. She has also marked the locations of an art institute near the university and of a chocolate shop on the Ferenc Liszt Square.

She has walked in these streets so many times in her imagination that they don't seem alien anymore. Their Hungarian names excite her each time she whispers them to herself but the excitement is soon replaced by angst; she fears that she might be disappointed by their commonness, that the aura she has created around them might dissipate, leaving her stranded in an unknown city, unable to face the failure of her quest.

On her Apple notebook she has a folder entitled LAURA & VOSS. The folder holds images of her Dad's recent paintings. Whenever she is bored she looks at them, struggling to understand the compulsion that forced him to paint them. It is true that she could have asked him herself, when she saw them being painted, but she knows that her Dad's answer would have fallen short. The trip to Budapest, she hopes, will solve the mystery and she will be able to see the paintings as her Dad must have seen them before he started painting them.

The computer doesn't hold a single item associated with her Mama—no emails, notes, photos or images. "I don't need them," she explains, "because I am in Budapest, the city where Mama was born and grew up."

*

On Wednesday, she packs her backpack with two apples, a water-bottle, a packet of nuts, her large map, folded neatly, two books, an umbrella and walks out of her room. In the kitchen she is greeted by two American college-students who are on a study-tour of Eastern Europe. She doesn't stop, waves goodbye and comes out. It's raining. She stops at the entrance to take her umbrella out but changes her mind. She covers her head with the hood of her jacket and walks.

Soon the rain stops and as she steps on the Chain Bridge the sun begins to shine again. She is surprised to see so many people. She shouldn't be. It's August, the month when Budapest is packed with tourists. She stops for a moment on the bridge and spots two large ferries approaching the bridge. One of them is bellowing dark smoke. The second blows a longish hoot. The tourists walking past her stop to watch the ferries. She steps away from the railing and before she can decide where to go she is caught up in the flow of tourists which deposits her on the Buda-side of the twin city.

For more than two hours she walks in the city instinctively following one or the other group, without ever stopping at a site for more than a few moments. Luckily the rain keeps away. It's a strange walk, without purpose or intent. For years afterwards she will try to recall it but fail to reconstruct even a single detail. "I was sleep-walking," she will say to her little daughter, who is yet to be born.

Feeling tired she proceeds to a bench in a little park on the Pest-side of the Chain Bridge. Not far from the bench is a toilet. She opens her palm and lets the old gipsy-looking woman pick whatever coins she is supposed to pay. As she comes out of the toilet the soft sun greets her. She goes back to bench, sits down, unties her shoe laces, opens her bag and takes out a large apple but just before she takes the first bite, something strange happens. A cold fluid-like feeling rises somewhere from inside her belly and she begins to cry. She picks up her backpack, holds it tight in her arms, and the weeping grows louder. Fortunately there isn't anyone around but for a couple of pigeons, who turn their wobbly heads to look at her then look away. As she bends to retrieve the apple that had fallen from her hand she sees the old woman holding a bouquet of red carnations.

She waits for the woman to shuffle past the large oak, then gets up, gathers her things and walks back to her apartment. In the apartment she takes off her shoes, gets into bed, covers herself from head to toe and goes to sleep in complete darkness.

*

That afternoon Maya sleeps for four or five hours. When she gets up it is already four o'clock. She has a shower, gets dressed, and exits the building and walks up to the apartment block she intended to visit in the morning. She knows the way and walks fast, eager not to be distracted. She stops in front of the building to confirm it is the right one, opens the door, climbs up the stairs to the third floor, finds the door with the number 14 and rings the bell. After waiting for a few seconds she rings again. Someone shuffles to the door. It opens. An old man in a shabby sweater is looking at her. His glasses hang around his neck. He is bald. His long lean face is covered by a full greyish beared. The look on the face frightens her. She says hello in Hungarian and introduces herself. The old man doesn't say anything in response. The bemused look on his face makes her even more uneasy.

It is time for her to initiate her plan B. She pulls out a sheet of paper from her pocket and gives it to him to read. The old man takes the sheet, tries to read it but gives it back to her without reading it.

"*Kerém* (Please)," she says in Hungarian again. The man takes the sheet back, puts on his glasses and reads.

"*Nem* (No)," he says handing back the sheet to her.

"*Kerém*," she says again, "only for a minute and no more," she adds in

English. "*Nem*," is the reply again. The old man shuts the door. She stands at the door and sits down on the floor. The door opens again. The old man looks at her. He raises his voice and says something in broken English. Go away! He threatens to call the police if she comes back.

She gets up, goes back to her apartment and watches a few episodes of *Friends* dubbed in Hungarian. She sleeps soundly, untroubled by dreams or by the noisy traffic outside the window she has forgotten to shut.

In the morning when she wakes up she knows what she has to do.

*

Just opposite the apartment block, she visited yesterday is a park with a skating rink. That's where her mother used to skate. She has seen the photos in the album. Her mother stands with her parents, holding their hands. In one of the photos she is sitting on the ice, looking at the camera, laughing. A white ribbon is tied to her longish hair. A little squirrel, nibbling at a pine kernel, sits nearby.

Maya finds a bench in the park near the rink and sits there watching and waiting. The block and the window of the apartment 14 are visible from where she sits. It is a wonderful autumn day; the bright sun feels soft on the skin. The woody smell of wet oaks and leaves grow around her, spreading a sense of hope. She truly believes that no problem is ever insoluble, that you only need to think about it without despair or desperation. That's what she does and the solution, literally, walks in.

His name is Vincent. Vincent Patrick Odongo, she finds out later. He stops, looks at her and asks if he can sit with her. "I wanted to speak to someone in English," he will tell her later. Both will agree it was good he asked, and that she moved her backpack to make space for him.

"Are you from Australia?" He asks. She answers yes and notices that the Qantas boarding pass, which she is using as a book mark, has slipped out of *Voss*. She tells him her name is Maya, and that she has come to Budapest to spend a few minutes in the apartment of her mother, who died a year ago. She tells him about her encounter with the old man who now lived in the apartment and that she didn't know what to do. He asks

101

her to come with him and leaving her outside the block he runs up the stairs. After ten or so minutes he pokes his head out of the window and calls her to come up. She enters, shakes hands with the old man and the three move to the kitchen table to talk. She explains the reason why she has come to Budapest. Vincent translates. The old man listens.

She tells them that when Zoscka, her Mama, was three, she saw from the window of that very kitchen, the Red Army tanks rumble on the street, their sirens bellowing. The windows had shaken, the glass cracked, and shots were fired. There was a tank with a number 320 painted on its side. It turned its barrel slowly and stopped pointing in the direction of the window. She watched and waited. Luckily the soldiers in the tank decided not to fire. The barrel returned to its previous position and the tank drove off.

Miklos, the old man, and Vincent get up, turn the noisy kettle on and make tea.

As they sip sweet black tea, it's decided that Maya, if she wants, can stay in the apartment for four days. Miklos during that time will go to live with his daughter in a village near Ocsa. The rent is cheap—sixty dollars for three nights. The money is to be paid in advance.

*

Maya stays in the apartment for six months instead of three nights. Until she has to leave suddenly.

She spends the first two weeks on her own but on the third, Vincent moves in with her. They both knew it would happen, but her falling in love with him continues to annoy her for a very long time.

Vincent is very likeable and lovable. He speaks three languages— Hungarian, Russian and English, which is novel for Maya. Her mono-lingualism seems utterly primitive in comparison, and she berates herself for giving up her French lessons.

He isn't particularly tall but standing beside him Maya feels like a little girl in one of Anderson's fairy tales. The recurring image in her dreams is of herself as a little parrot finch perched on the outstretched palm of Vincent. He is strong, all muscle and no fat, and the sheer agility he displays captivates her. A young man in total command of his body, an African David, ready to hurl his disc into the deepest realms of the universe.

He was born in the city of Ibadan, a few hundred kilometres north of Lagos. He was the eldest of six siblings, the rest all girls. He had come to Hungary to finish a medical degree in orthopaedics. Eight years of hard work, shunting between Budapest and Ibadan, where his mother Thelma Louise waited for him to return.

But his first love is football, or "soccer as you call it in Australia". He is quite good at it. Scouts from several reputed clubs in Europe have shown interest in him. He invites Maya to watch him train with one of the local clubs and shows her various tricks, trying to impress her. He also takes her to meet Aniko, the daughter of the famous Puskas, the Galloping Major, and shows her a video of Puskas's ten best goals.

*

They are embarrassed the first time they make love. It isn't rushed but seemed contrived, a kind of transaction. Maya is grateful to Vincent for convincing Miklos to let her stay in the apartment and Vincent wants to make her feel at home in a strange city. Maya has told him about the incident in the Roosevelt Park and he doubts if she has fully recovered. He wants her to feel safe and, most of all, loved.

For a couple of weeks after the first night, they try their utmost not to be alone with each other in a room and although they spend a lot of time together, mostly walking in the city, they wait in hope for the embarrassment of the first night to turn into a more tender feeling.

For Vincent the change occurs when Maya starts telling him about her father Harry and her Hungarian mother Zoscka. She tells him how her father was a famous painter and her mother an accomplished sculptor, and that they lived in a small farming town of Braidwood, not far from the capital Canberra. She has *Google Earth* on hand and she shows him various maps with her friendly river and the little farm house on its rocky eastern bank. Near the farm house is a small shearing shed which has been converted into two studios—hers larger than his, because as a sculptor she needed more space to mess about, but also because she was the boss.

"She was very beautiful," Maya tells him, "very intelligent and sensitive. She knew how to spot beauty and make it shine with just a few slight touches of her magical hands. "You are blessed," Dad used to tell her. To which her reply was always the same, "Yes, I know."

Zoscka saw Harry's paintings and told him that he was wasting his time, producing useless imitations of great masters of the past. Harry was impressed by her honesty and her desire to see him succeed. He went back to the place where he was born and grew up looking for stories whispered to him by rocks, rivers, plants and birds. But instead of painting landscapes he started making intriguing portraits in which a human figure was present but so entwined with the landscape it required special effort to spot it. Like fossils the figure was hidden in the landscape but once it had been identified it came to life radiating the joy of its presence.

Maya shows Vincent photos of the house and the studio, all stored in different, neatly labelled, folders in her notebook. "Our hills are short, stubby, and shy," she tells him, "they loll so very close to the ground that you feel as if they want to disappear into the deep folds of mother earth. That's why our rivers are flat, capricious and miserly; the forests scraggy, dry, and oily, ready to catch fire at will, and when they burn, they burn like hell."

"And what about the sea?" he asks her. "I hate it," she says without ever explaining the reason.

"You sound like your mother," he says. "Not at all," she replies, "I am my father's daughter."

"Is she really her father's daughter?" Vincent often wonders, unable to decide why Maya is so different from the many other women he has slept with. He liked being with women and found them gracious and forgiving. Many wanted to talk, but mostly about things he found trivial, as if talking was foreplay or post-coital indulgence. For Maya talking is a serious transaction in which words are too precious to be thrown around without care or conviction. She speaks less but whatever she says is uttered with passion, and the passion isn't expressed in the loudness of her voice or by repeating the thought like an automaton, but in a firm whispering voice that assures him she isn't interested in picking a fight or winning an argument. "It's her passion," he tells himself, "that I like the most." Falling in love is a mess he has come to believe, yet with Maya, he allows himself to be carried away hoping however that he will either grow out of it or that Maya herself will find an excuse to end the affair.

He is wrong, because this twenty-five year old woman from Australia, who teaches geography in a college, is special. The fragility she, at times, displays is deceptive. She possesses, he quickly surmises, a solid inner core revealed by a glint in her large hazel eyes, that convinces him that once she has made up her mind she will accomplish the task with conviction, grace and humility.

*

"This is the first painting my Dad did after he and Zoscka came to Australia," Maya tells him showing the painting on the screen of her Apple notebook.

Vincent looks. A boat in a lake and in the sky above, a large moon with a woman's face; her slender body painted in a crimson summer dress is stretched across the sky. That the woman is Zoscka, he recognises immediately, but what catches his attention is a little peacock perched on the edge of the boat, its neck extended upward as if trying to reach the moon with its ivory-white beak.

"Two years ago when Zoscka was diagnosed with terminal cancer of the uterus," continues Maya, "Harry began to create a sequence of paintings called the *Dreams of Johann Ulrich Voss*. He painted Zoscka in each of the twelve paintings, turning her into Voss's Laura. Zoscka died ten months ago but Harry is still painting the sequence."

Vincent asks her about Voss and Laura and Maya hands him *Voss*, the book with blue and yellow stickers. She tells him about Ludwig Leichhardt, the German explorer, and how he was transformed into Voss in the novel. Like Leichhardt, Voss didn't return from the expedition, killed somewhere in the vast desert. Laura, a young woman in Sydney, his great love, accompanies him on the expedition, not physically but in his dreams, as if she were painted inside his head, heart and soul, ready to seep out each time he decides to shut his eyes. He becomes so accustomed to her presence that he sees her riding along with him on her own chestnut horse. At night when he falls asleep she sits with him watching over him like an angel, and when sleep eludes him, she sings German songs to him in the unblemished voice of his mother.

Vincent looks at the second painting: a broad floodplain of a dry river littered with thousands of small rounded stones; the blinding whiteness stained here and there with lumps of red and yellow ochre. Stuck in the flat plain is a white horse, visible only because of the streaks of dirt painted on its left side. The face of the horse is turned back to look at the viewer; its large eyes are clotted with a cluster of flies. On the horse a woman in a red dress, not in the saddle, but floating just above it; the feet bare, delicate like fish in a bowl. Her face is hidden from the viewer, but from the shape of the head one can imagine that she is angelic; her curly dark auburn hair flows from her head like streams. Near the horse holding the strap, an arm of a man, hairy, sweaty and marked with scabby spots; on the ground near the arm a little peacock pecking at a large white pebble.

The painting stuns Vincent into silence. Speaking seems impossible, rude, sacrilegious. Only Maya can be heard speaking as she shows him painting after painting. They are figurative but not truly naturalistic. The figures are often disproportionate, sometimes large, sometimes small, but always ungrounded, always floating in the air.

In each painting Zoscka in her red dress is accompanied by a blue-necked peacock. Only in a couple of paintings Voss appears full and complete, otherwise his presence is limited to an arm, a hand, a pair of eyes or just a head looking away from the viewer. In one rare painting they appear together, floating above the reddened mounds of rocks spiked with grass. She is lying on her back; her red hair streaming down under the imaginary bed of clouds. Voss is lying on his side, his right arm stretched across her body touching the invisible pubic mound. The painting shows only his right eye and a part of his ruddy beard. The face is lean, bony, pointed—the face of Jesus.

"You are right," Vincent hears Maya speak, "Harry's Voss looks like Jesus. Jesus in love."

*

"Do you miss her?" she asks Vincent one early morning. They are still in bed, feeling kind, warm and gracious in each other's company. Maya understands that this isn't the best time to ask the question but hopes that closeness they have begun to display may usher in an honest answer. He doesn't reply.

"You must miss your little boy," she says suspecting that the word might both surprise and irritate him.

"Yes, I miss Phillip," he replies. He looks at the photo near his wallet on the bedside table and assumes that Maya has seen it. She has. One night she got up for a glass of water and as she was about to put it down on the table she knocked his wallet off. The photo showed itself when she picked it up. She took the photo back in to the kitchen for a closer look, leaving Vincent asleep. It was a normal family photo taken in a studio. His wife was standing to his left. Tall and slim, she was wearing a blue skirt and a white blouse. Her hair was cut short and there was a silvery nose-bud studded in her beautiful nose. Vincent stood tall, smiling, carrying on his right arm their little boy, a year or so old, dressed in a white shirt and shorts with a little golden cross in a chain round his neck. Maya had read the date on the back of the photo. "He must be six or seven now," she whispered to herself. She had walked back to the table and left the photo outside the wallet.

She had got back into bed and fallen asleep immediately, which surprised her, her arm wrapped around him.

"Phillip will turn seven this year," Vincent speaks. "On October 16. My wife's name is Mary Anne. She teaches English in a high school. I know her from my school days. We went to the same university. That we got married didn't surprise anyone. She is very kind and has stayed behind to look after my mother and my sisters. I talk to her every week and send them money. I want her to come to Budapest, but she doesn't want to leave the family alone. I go home for a month each year. I phone every other day. I am always in touch, always thinking about them."

"Even when you are with me, making love to me," Maya wants to ask but doesn't. There is no need.

If she feels betrayed, disgraced or used, she doesn't show it. Perhaps she doesn't feel like that at all. At least not now. But what about guilt or shame? She assumes that like her he must feel guilty too—guilty of stealing and lying, of being selfish and weak.

"Do you love me?" She doesn't want to ask that either, because if he asks her the same question she will struggle to find an honest reply. To say no, is incorrect, to say yes utterly untrue.

*

After that unsettling early morning conversation, they don't see each other for a week, but as often happens, they bump into one another in a coffee shop, not entirely accidentally, and resolve that it is foolish to avoid each other.

Maya begins attending Vincent's training. She sits alone at the edge of the soccer field and watches him play. The urge to draw emerges slowly but once she starts, it's hard to stop. And that's when she feels she is beginning to fall in love.

During the day she works in a small art gallery in Buda, not far from the Church of Mary Magdalene. Working in the galleries isn't new for her. As a student in Canberra she had been employed part-time in a number of studios and galleries either as an administrator or a receptionist. On a number of occasions she had even helped to set up exhibitions and edit a catalogue or two. The gallery in Buda is rather small, targetted at American and English tourists. There are a few nice paintings by contemporary Hungarian artists, but most attractive works are pieces of pottery and sculptures made of stained glass.

Evenings they often cook dinner together; Vincent cooking and she mainly helping with cutting, chopping and slicing. On Tuesdays and Thursdays Vincent is on night duty in the hospital. Maya spends these nights watching television or movies in an old cinema theatre that screens old, almost 'ancient', European films. If she feels too lonely, she phones Vincent and joins him in the hospital, sleeping in a little bed in the room for the interns.

"I have fallen in love Dad," she writes to Harry in an email. The reply is equally short: "Wonderful. I'll pray for you." In her next email she sends Harry copies of three sketches of Vincent. The reply again is brief: "The sketches are good. They need more work. Do you want me to transfer some money into your account?"

*

On one cold morning in January, Maya packs her suitcase and leaves. The reason isn't the sudden onslaught of snow and cold icy wind but something more urgent. Vincent is in Berlin at a conference. He had asked her to come with him, but she had refused.

She phones Miklos to thank him for letting her stay in the apartment and asks him if she can take off one of the white lacy curtains on the kitchen window, promising to leave money for him to buy a new curtain. "No problem," he says and invites her to come again next year. "Don't forget to bring Harry next time."

She goes to Vincent's apartment and leaves a packet in his mailbox. It contains her copy of *Voss* and a little fluffy wombat.

On the train to Vienna she decides she isn't quite ready to return home. She needs time to regain control over her feelings. In the train she meets Sarah, a musicologist from Scotland, who is researching a thesis on a Soviet composer. She is renting a large room in a block of apartments on Singerstraße. She tells Maya the room is big enough for two and that she is welcome to stay, but Maya declines the offer opting to stay in a small hotel not far from Singerstraße. Opposite the hotel is an English bookshop run by two women. One of them hails from Perth and is overjoyed to see a fellow countrywoman. On a notice board in the bookshop Maya finds an ad placed by an elderly woman who wants a companion to practice her English with. Maya phones the woman and gets the job.

Frau Fritza Bauer lives alone in an apartment opposite the building that houses the Freud Museum. Despite her old age she is quite active, still publishing illustrated books for children and young adults.

She offers to take Maya to her GP, who confirms that Maya is eight-weeks pregnant. She is told that both she and her baby are fine and that apart from a month-long course of iron supplements she doesn't need anything special. She is told to go for long walks, enjoy the fresh air and be happy.

Vincent calls her on her mobile but she doesn't reply. His text messages are read and promptly deleted. The same happens to his emails. Her stubborn silence brings an end to his calls.

"I love him," she tells herself, "but not enough to make him leave his family." She doesn't want to reply to Vincent's messages because she is afraid that the news of her pregnancy might force him to make hasty and unwise decisions. She thinks she will be happy bringing up the baby alone and is convinced that her dad would welcome the baby and help her look after her. The presence of a little girl, and she was sure that the baby would be a girl, will bring joy to a house that felt so utterly abandoned after the death of Zoscka.

Maya spends two months in Vienna. There are times when she is terribly unhappy and lonely. She misses Vincent. She wants him to be with her; to make love to her with their baby inside her; put his ear on her tummy and hear the little creature splash around like a fish; talk to the little fish and sing her songs and rhythms of Ibadan or Timbuktu; hold her in his arms and tell her that she is beautiful. At times she misses him so much it physically hurts; her heart seizes up and a state of breathlessness follows that forces her to flap her arms and feet as if she were trying to save herself from drowning. After such moments of utter desperation she rings his number either to hear his voice speaking the recorded message or just to feel him breathe.

She has always found the intensity with which her dad loved Zoscka incomprehensible, mad, even uncanny. "No one can ever love anyone like that," she used to say. Her mama would just laugh. "People like him do," she would reply, hinting that she herself wasn't one of them. Zoscka's love for Harry was more practical, matter-of-fact, normal, almost routine. Maya is convinced, and this thought troubles her, that if Harry had died first, Zoscka wouldn't have felt the need to do something akin to Harry's Voss and Laura paintings. She definitely would have grieved for him and grieved for years perhaps but the grief like her love for Harry would have remained subdued, subsumed by the ordinariness of her everyday life.

She also begins to doubt her Dad's intentions as well. Not his love for Zoscka but the intensity with which it has been expressed. Although it has given birth to wonderful works of art, she feels that Harry was so consumed by his love and grief that the only way to survive was to let that grief pour out. By painting Zoscka as Laura again and again he is trying to wash her out of his system. Perhaps that is the reason why he decided either to erase Voss from the paintings completely or to keep his presence in them limited to an arm, a head or a peacock.

*

In the last week of March Maya returns home. Harry meets her at the airport. The words following a big hug are: "Welcome home, you two".

At home she shows him the lacy white curtain she has brought from Zoscka's apartment. She tells him she has decided to call the baby girl Aniko. He doesn't ask why but she nevertheless tells him about Puskas, the famous soccer player, and his daughter. "Is she alright?" he asks. "Of course," she replies and shows him the ultrasound image of Aniko floating inside her.

A few weeks after Aniko is born, Maya and Harry finish the first draft of a graphic novella. The book is called *Zoscka's Window*. It tells the story of a four-year old girl living in a Budapest apartment. The girl in the pictures resembles both Zoscka and Aniko.

When Aniko is six months old, Maya writes a letter to Vincent. With the letter she sends a photo of Aniko and an imprint of her right hand on a sheet of paper. She explains to Vincent that although she doesn't need any help raising Aniko, she will be grateful if he keeps in touch. Aniko, she says, will one day want to meet her handsome father. She tells him that if ever he gets a chance to travel to Australia he is welcome to visit them and spend some time with Aniko. She takes special care to remind him that Aniko was born on the eleventh day of September, which is her birthday as well. She apologises to him for stealing a photo of him and Phillip from one of his albums. The photo is for Aniko. "Please tell Phillip," she writes, "not now but whenever appropriate, about Aniko, his half-sister."

For a while she doesn't receive anything in reply but after six months a packet arrives from Vincent which contains her copy of *Voss*. No letter, no note. Not a single word.

Heidegger's Hammer

"Did you know that Martin Heidegger, the grandfather of Martin Heidegger, the philosopher, was a master cobbler?" Iliya asked me one evening. The puzzled look on my face made him smile.

I had met Iliya in a train on my trip back from Klin, a small town eighty or so kilometres northwest of Moscow. It was my third visit to the Tchaikovsky Museum. My last trip had been in December, just a week before Christmas. The one before happened in June in the midst of one of the hottest summers. On that trip I had decided that I would return to Klin in the autumn to enjoy the melancholic colours of the surrounding park overgrown with oaks, birches and lindens.

Touched by the magical hand of autumn, the wooden house looked magnificent. Its bluish exterior studded with sash and round-headed windows lined with white frames created the dreamy state of a fairy tale. I saw the famous flashlight-shaped balcony capped with a spear-like little tower. Inside the balcony near a large latticed window stood a round table where the famous composer used to sit for his tea.

I also saw the large pond and lingered for a few moments near the bronze statue of Tchaikovsky seated on a bench planted on a granite slab. The composer sat on the edge of the bench leaving enough space for the visitors to sit with him and share the view. I walked on paved and unpaved tracks in the park listening to his music coming out of the speakers installed along the way.

It was a wonderful autumn day. The air had a tinge of chill but the light was soft and the colours not too bright and restful.

In the evening returning to Moscow, I found the train carriage crowded with weekenders returning from their dachas carrying buckets of unwashed potatoes, carrots and mushrooms. I couldn't find a seat for some time. I would have very much liked to sit down, to put my feet up on the opposite seat and rest. However, there is something special when one travels standing in a train. The whole body becomes part of the motion, swaying forwards and backwards as the train slows down and picks up. But most of all, standing up helps to look around. That's how I spotted Iliya in the coach.

He was sitting near the window. A bald man with a sketching pad in his hand. He was drawing with sharp quick movements of his left hand. The short charcoal stick in his long knobbly fingers swished across the face of the sheet, stopped for a moment and got busy again—an old woman with a silk scarf; a young boy holding a cage with a yellow bird; a man with red curly hair holding the hand of his pregnant wife; a bucket with fish; and a bunch of tulips peeping through the unzipped mouth of a rucksack on the back of a militiaman.

I stood for a while. Tired and bored I looked around for a seat. Luckily an old woman moved to make some space for me to sit. It was next to Iliya. By then he had stopped drawing. I wanted to talk to him but didn't know where to start, so I pulled a book out of my rucksack instead.

"So you read Dostoevsky?" I heard him ask.

"Are you a painter?" I answered with my own question.

"Dostoevsky is so very Russian. Do you really understand him?"

"I don't know," I said. "He is difficult but I am getting used to his style and long sentences. May I have a look at your sketches?"

*

Iliya Ginsburg owned a small dacha in Yamuga, a few kilometres north of Klin. The three-room peasant-hut stood alone on the elevated southern bank of a river that cut through a thick pine grove. One of the rooms with a large window opening to the river had been turned into a studio. In the centre of the room stood a large rustic pine table covered with the usual paraphernalia of a painter's studio.

"Are you a Moskovitch?" I asked Iliya.

"No", he replied. "I was born in Leningrad, a few years before the war. But my wife comes from Moscow. She is a photographer. That's her."

A figure in black and white holding in her lap a yellow vase with purple flowers painted on its round belly. *Yellow Vase with My Wife*, the caption read.

114

I looked around. There were no other paintings. The walls were empty. Just one portrait of a yellow vase with his wife.

However, what amazed me most were the two potter's wheels in the corner. One of them was still covered with lumps of white and yellow clay. The shelves were cluttered with finished and half-finished objects. There were several vases quite similar to the one his wife was holding in the painting.

"I am a potter," Iliya said, "and sculpting and painting are just hobbies."

A few minutes later he took me to a small shed at the back of the house. I had never before seen such a congregation of odd things: sea shells and snail shells, stumps of trees, crooked branches, drift wood, rocks, pebbles, crystals, pine cones, nests, fossils, feathers, bells, pitchers, pots, leaves painted and unpainted, ropes, cups, vases, rags, barbed wire, boxes, broken vinyl records.

There was a well in front of the house and beside it stood a wooden bench. This is where we would often sit and talk. He with his pipe and I with a cup of tea and my *zenith* camera ready to take a photo.

"The world comes to us in the form of things," he once said. This, I'll find out later, was his first paraphrase of Heidegger. His German was bad and he didn't know English at all. We weren't sure if Heidegger was available in Russian. Maybe that's why we decided to read Heidegger together; Iliya read to me in German, translating the passages into Russian. I read out the same passages in English translating them into Russian.

One day he showed me a list of words he had read in *Being and Time*. Here is the list: hammer, plane, needle, shoe, clock, tongs, cars, vehicles, red arrows, gloves, knots in handkerchief, house, rooms, books, field, clothes, boat, piece of chalk, wood, a pair of pliers, a watch, an apple and a piece of bread, rose, shrub, beech, tree, spruce, lizard, wasp, granite, limestone, rock, pebble, two buckets, two pine needles, jug, axe, church bells, candles, chimney, Mercedes, Volkswagen, door, forest clearing, beetle, grass, blade of grass, well, milk, water, thistle, leaf, hawk, radio set, logs, picture, rifle, hat.

"Heidegger," he said, "looks at the world like a sculptor, touching it with his eyes and mind and the world touches him back. His things seem to show and announce themselves. They are lit up or over-shadowed; they are obstinate and obtrusive. They regard us, flash at us, solicit us, become conspicuous, ask for our concern, hide and conceal from us. They are animated. They look at us and demand our attention and we are unable to ignore them." He was enchanted by Heidegger, by his beguiling ability to handle and describe things and the world we live in.

One winter afternoon as the snow flakes floated silently through the sky and fell on us to melt away instantly, he suddenly pronounced in German, "*Welt ist auch Dasein* (*Dasein* too is world) and asked me if I knew what the phrase meant. However, before I could advance a sensible answer he began explaining.

"Take for instance the vase, the one you saw in the painting. I made it from clay and water; I first mounted the clay on the wheel. My hands grasped its wet clayey softness. I moulded it and the clay moulded my hands. That's how I came to be in this world with the vase, the clay and the quarry near Klin. I made the vase for Anna. When I was making it I was thinking about her and of Lena whose hair she was combing. This vase takes me to the world, the one in which I am already in, but of which I am still not fully aware.

"I put the vase in the furnace. There it cooks like a loaf of bread. Then I paint on it. The painted vase is then painted into Anna's portrait. The portrait is seen by my friends and by people who remain unknown to me. Strange things happen to me and the vase and to other people who see the painting. The world is no longer the same after I have made the vase and put it there on the shelf with the other vases and pots."

I responded with a quizzical smile after he had finished his monologue.

"You know, I have written a poem about the vase Anna Andreevna is holding in your painting," I said after a pause.

"So, you are a poet as well."

"Not really, I just write short rhymes to pass time, nothing special. But I like reading poetry."

"What are you reading these days?"

"Mayakovsky."

"Mayakovsky? That's really interesting. He wrote a lovely poem called *You have to be kind to Horses*. Do you know the poem? Nice to hear that you like him. Not many do. For them it's either Pushkin or Blok."

"I like them too," I wanted to tell him, "but I enjoy the arrogance of Mayakovsky. Both Pushkin and Blok are so disciplined in their strict rhymed quatrains. Mayakovsky breaks the imposition by inventing sliding, cascading rhymes, which roll over you like waves."

I didn't tell Iliya any of this. In fact the short time we were together, most of the talking was done by Iliya. I usually kept quiet, knowing that the role of a patient listener suited me best. Iliya understood this at once and enjoyed my silent presence. It gave him the confidence to tell me things he had not told to anyone. He came to believe I wouldn't let his words go astray.

Now when I think about it, our friendship, if one can call that short acquaintance friendship, was quite strange. He was much older than I. while his daughter Lena, was only a couple of years younger. A few times he even tried to get something going between her and me. He soon realised, however, that it would not happen. Shy, bookish, indecisive and introverted, I was too boring for her.

A few months later, in April, I think, I got a phone call from Lena. "Papa has sent a packet for you," she said.

"From where," I asked.

"Berlin," she replied.

Lena lived with her mother on the eighth floor of one of Moscow's seven towers, the infamous wedding cakes of Stalin. From Lena I found out that her mother had left Iliya. "They were having problems," she said. "It isn't easy to live with papa you know," she added, and from the sad smile on her face I ascertained that the separation was final.

The packet contained a letter:

Berlin, 8th August 1978

Dear K,

I know that this letter from Berlin will come as a surprise. Right now I am sitting in a park writing this letter. It is getting dark and I need to finish the letter as soon as possible. I am not sure what is going to happen next. I am confused, uncertain. Never mind. So here it is.

I have returned this very morning from Badenweiler. I am sure you'll recognise this name. In Berlin a strange thing happened to me. At the Rosa-Luxemburg Platz station I met a young German actor. She spoke Russian. "I am a big fan of Chekhov," she said and went on to describe the famous Efros production of The Cherry Orchard *at the Taganka Theatre in which Vysotsky played Lopakhin. "Lets go to Badenweiler, I'll show you the hotel room in which Olga Knipper saw Chekhov breathe his last." I knew it was risky for a Russian to travel in this country. But she had contacts. In no time an appropriate invitation was obtained for me and a proper visa was stamped in my passport.*

We took a night train from the Potsdam Station and reached Baden Baden early in the morning. Dostoevsky, your favourite, spent a few weeks in Baden and Baden and lost lots of money in one of the gambling establishments there. He was a compulsive gambler and didn't mind leaving his young wife Anna alone in a hotel in Berlin. You should read the letters he wrote her. So weak and pathetic.

We spent the day in Baden Baden and in the evening took a train to Basel. I am enclosing a few sketches of Hanna. She is small. Not tiny but small, and shapely in a fullish way. Looking at her is not enough. I always feel the need to touch her. Not that I have touched her but I know that it would be wonderful to hold her, then lift her off her feet and take her to bed.

I almost forgot, there is one more, quite special thing about her face. Her left ear is longer, and a little thicker than the right, and a tiny horizontal scar at the end of the left ear accentuates the disparity.

We found the hotel Badenweiler without much trouble and saw the room and the windows near which Olga Knipper must have stood confused and helpless, watching Anton die. There was a small cafe opposite the hotel. It served sweet Turkish coffee and lovely cherry cakes.

"Let us see where else we can go," Hanna said in the evening, spreading her small tourist map of the Black Forest on the table. I looked at the map and saw Todtnauberg. "Is this the same Todtnauberg?" I asked. "I didn't know you were interested in the great philosopher," Hanna replied.

We took a popular walking track in Badenweiler and walked up to the road going to Schonau where we boarded a bus. At Schonau we hired bikes and cycled slowly along the road to Todtnauberg. Our conversation was similar to the ride, slow and tentative, punctuated with pauses and unanswered questions.

Hanna's mother died a year after Hanna was born. The life after the concentration camps wasn't easy. She was exhausted and didn't want to live. The cancer finished her. After her death, Hanna's father deposited her in an orphanage and disappeared. "I learnt Russian from a Russian teacher at the refuge. She knew Nabokov and seemed to have done typing for him. At least that's what she told me." We saw the hut, Heidegger's hut ....

And the letter stopped. I looked for the next page, but couldn't find it. I searched inside the packet but there was nothing there. I phoned Lena but she too didn't know anything about it. I showed her the sketches of Hanna.

"She looks interesting. Who is she?"

"Hanna," I said, "a German actor," and told Lena about her father's trip to Badenweiler and Todtnauberg.

In the packet I found a few sketches of the hut and a well. Paul Celan describes the well and the star-die in his poem *Todtnauberg*.

The sketch showed a wooden log and standing over it a metallic shaft with a star-die and a long straight tap with water dripping from it. 'The Spring' the caption read.

I later found out that the well in Celan's poem is in reality a spring. Strictly speaking it is not even a spring. I am told that a mountain creek that runs on the eastern side of the hut is its real source.

*

For almost a year I didn't hear anything from Iliya, Lena or her mother. One day in August I received a small note from Iliya's wife, in which she asked me to come to the dacha the following weekend. Lena met me at the station and as we walked to the dacha she told me that Iliya had defected and was now living in Basel. "The KGB is very angry with us. Did they come looking for you as well?"

"No", I replied, "I've been away in India. I only got back a week ago."

"You should be careful," she warned me.

"*Vot kakoi svoloch* (What a pig?)." Lena's mother was quite upset. "To leave us in this situation. Did he tell you anything? Did he warn you? You two were so close."

"Not really", I replied, "I hardly knew him."

"Who is Hanna?" She asked me. "Lena told me that Iliya met an actress in Berlin."

I recounted the story of the unfinished letter, the sketches and of the trip to Badenweiler and Todtnauberg.

"O Well. He is gone, leaving the mess behind. I have been sacked from my job and all the other newspapers have been warned not to hire me."

I left the dacha confused, unable to say anything sensible. On the way back I kept thinking about Iliya's unfinished letter. What was worrying him in Berlin that morning? Why didn't he finish the letter? If he did finish it, why didn't he send the whole letter? Was it an oversight or a secret message? Was he trying to tell me something? Did the KGB open the letter?

A few months after meeting Iliya's wife at the dacha, I bumped into Lena in the foyer of the Mayakovsky Drama Theatre.

"Nice to see you again," she said. We miss you, you know."

"I was expecting you to call or send a note. Is everything alright? How is Mama?"

"She is going to Tbilisi to do a book on the wild flowers in the Caucusus. We are selling our dacha. Mama doesn't need it and I don't want to go there. Papa has left so many things in the dacha. We don't know what to do with them? Is there anything you want to keep? Why don't you come and have a look?"

I phoned her the following weekend asking her if it would be alright for me to come to the dacha. As usual she met me at the station and we walked to the dacha talking about this and that. She was studying literature at the Herzen Institute. She told me about one of her friends who was working on the translation of one of Kalidas's Sanskrit poems.

"Do you know Sanskrit?" She asked.

"Just a little," I replied. Lena wanted me to meet her friend and if possible help her with the translation.

I spent a few hours in Iliya's shed rummaging through his pottery and found a few strange looking chamber pots. One of them had Stalin's face painted on it. It made me laugh. There was a little note tied to the handle of' the pot. It read: 'Don't be scared to piss'.

More interesting, however, were a series of Russian *matryoshkas*. One of them showed a set of grotesque monkeys with human faces. The first face was that of Lenin, and hooked onto his long penis was a smiling Stalin. Attached to Stalin's own short thing was the figure of Field Marshall Brezhnev, the General Secretary. In the lap of the General Secretary sat a haggard babushka with the caption 'Mother Russia'.

In the seventies Stalin had suddenly found some acceptance in the official circles. His name began to reappear in history books and newspapers. I remember the film epic *Osvobozhgenie* (*Liberation*) that told the Soviet story of the Great War. Each appearance of Stalin on the screen was greeted with applause. There were a few who even stood up to salute him.

"Can I take these?" I asked Lena.

"Are you sure? You'll get into trouble."

"I know but I have contacts. I'll manage."

I took the chamber pot and the *matryoshka* with three monkeys home. One of my Indian friends had an acquaintance in the Indian High Commission. Through the diplomatic mailbag we were able to smuggle it out of Russia.

A week before leaving Moscow and returning to India, I phoned Lena to say goodbye.

"I've got something for you. It's good that you phoned. Papa left a few things especially for you. I found them in his desk."

Lena gave me a wooden hammer and a blue notebook in Iliya's handwriting. The notebook showed how serious Iliya was about his Heidegger. It contained quotes from Heidegger, Iliya's sometimes quite idiosyncratic comments, a few sketches, some Russian postage stamps and a Russian translation of Celan's *Death Fugue*.

My small library has a bilingual edition of Celan's poems. I must have bought the book in India and I am surprised that I haven't lost it. In that book on the page with the poem *Death Fugue* in German there are lines written in Russian enclosed in square brackets. The Russian translation is in my handwriting:

Dein goldenes Haar Margarete
Твои золотые волосы Маргарита
Dein aschenes Haar Sulamith
Твои пепельные волосы Суламифь

A folded sheet of paper is glued on the facing page with the poem in English translation. The sheet has Iliya's brief comment in Russian:

Who is Sulamith? I'll have to retrieve my copy of the Old Testament. Will I find the name there? His poems have no punctuations, no stops, no colons. A flow, a steady flow, an overflow. Repetitions. I remember Anna reading Lorca. There were so many repetitions in the poem. "A lament," she said. That's how women lament. Repeating the same words over and over. Women give birth and look after the dead, wash them, dress them and leave them to be taken away. The lament. The wailing going up and down like a dead gull in the dark waves.

*

In the late eighties before leaving for Australia I packed up my books, notes, and music records in a few wooden boxes and left them with my brother. Being an officer in the army, he had to move to a new city every three or so years and it would have been hard for him to truck them around. He, as it happened, deposited the boxes with his in-laws in Delhi. In the early nineties when I finally decided to settle down in Australia, I asked my brother to send me the boxes.

For a while I didn't hear anything from him about the boxes. He always seemed to forget mentioning them. I was convinced that something untoward must have happened to them. Then one day, almost a year after my initial request, I received a letter from the Australian customs office in Sydney. I was asked to come to Sydney where an officer told me that the inspectors had confiscated a packet from India sent to me. It contained remains of a wooden hammer, infested with termites. "We had to destroy it," the officer told me.

My brother's explanation was simple. The boxes, he wrote to me later, were put on the roof of a shed and forgotten. When, after receiving my letter, he opened them, there was nothing left of the contents except powder and dust. Even the vinyl records had crumbled. A few bits of a wooden hammer, some note books and a few reproductions of Chagall's paintings had survived. "I am sorry," he wrote, "But you are an Australian now. You won't have any need for your Russian things. Am I right?"

No, my brother wasn't right and I am sure he knew that too. The Russianness which I had acquired during those long nine years doesn't wash away so easily. The traces always remain. Look at the paper from which my ten-year old son has tried hard to rub off the sketch of the bird he drew a few minutes ago. The image of the bird has disappeared but the effort to erase the image hasn't. In fact it is more visible than the image itself. Nothing ever disappears completely.

On that fateful day in August 1978 Iliya disappeared suddenly along with the remains of his letter. That unfinished letter announced the appearance of Hanna, the German actor. But she too was lost from the story. For a long time, I assumed that she was in Basel with Iliya. But was she really with him? Maybe she just appeared on the horizon like a shooting star, showed the way to Iliya and vanished. However, her presence in Iliya's story as a fairy godmother does not satisfy me. The mystery of the moment intrigues me because I have come to believe that it could have somehow changed Iliya's life forever.

*

In 1993, almost fifteen years after the events I have described above, I went to Moscow to attend a conference. On one Sunday I caught a train to Yamuga and went to Iliya's dacha. I couldn't find it. In its place stood a nice three-storeyed Scandinavian villa. As I walked around the villa I saw the remains of the shed and a few pieces of pottery covered in mud and lichen. I knocked at the door. A little girl came out. She looked at me, heard my question and went in to call her babushka. I was asked to come in and was offered tea and spicy gingerbread. Babushka knew Lena and Anna Andreevna. Anna had died a few years ago in Georgia, hit by a truck as she was crossing the street.

"What about Lena?" I asked.

"Lena, yes, let me think," she waited for a few minutes, "I think she left Russia. I am told she met a Dutch sailor in Tallinn and went with him to South Africa." I also asked her about Iliya but she didn't know anything about him.

"May I have a look in the shed?" I asked her.

"Of course, but you won't find anything in it. Leonid, my son, got rid of the junk. He is planning to build a garage there."

I thanked her for the tea and went out to inspect the shed. I walked around it and gathered a few pieces of pottery, some of which, I think, were the remains of Iliya's vases. I brought them to Canberra and perhaps it was then that I decided to write to my brother in India inquiring about my Russian 'things'.

In those days I was working on an essay about the semiotics of still-life painting and had begun to re-read Heidegger. I discovered that my memory without any conscious effort on my part was reproducing comments which, I was certain I had read in Iliya's note books. Here is one of them:

Der hammer, hammern, der pickhammer, der meißelhammer, der klauenhammer.[Hammer. I don't know why this hammer fascinates me. Was Heidegger too fascinated by hammers? He loved the workshop in his father's church. The bells. People praying warmed by each other's breathing. But why hammer, why not a pen or a piece of chalk? Why was hammer always ready-to-hand (*zuhanden*)? When he hammered a nail the hammer was *zuhanden* but when he inserted the word hammer into his dense thought did it remain *zuhanden*? What happens to things when we begin to think about them? Do they remain the same in thoughts as well as in images? And what about memory? Why does it cling to things?]

Yes, what happens to things when memory, like a marooned boat, drops anchors around them? Is it able to catch the whole thing in the net or does part of it always slip away, disappearing forever leaving behind just a ripple?

The Quartz Hill

"I am Alice too," she says, "Alice Walker." She gets up, kicks off her shoes, runs to the water and slows down. The evening air is cool and the sky peachy from the fading sun. The other Alice wants to follow her, but somehow can't force herself to get up. She just sits and watches the other Alice run and walk or just stand, her head tilted, exposing the soft bronzy flesh of the neck and shoulder. Why? She wonders. Is it because she has herself always felt caged, tied down? Before she met Alice, she had seemed quite happy with her predicament. In fact it never felt like a predicament. So what happened?

She first saw Alice in the market one evening, bending down to touch a piece of pottery on a table. She picked it up, turned her head and that's when the shutter was pressed. Pure instinct. She couldn't control herself. Feeling ashamed she decided to go up to Alice to apologise. She didn't have to. "This isn't very good, is it?" Alice pointed at the little bowl. She wanted to say yes, but by then Alice had placed the bowl back, looked at her and they started walking; came out of the market, and sat down on a bench under a fig.

She told Alice that she was a freelance photographer, and that if Alice was really interested in pottery she would take her to one of her Portuguese friends, an expert, who could assist her in acquiring a few really good pieces. Alice thanked her for the offer and said that she wasn't particularly interested in pottery; that she was a student too poor to afford an authentic piece. Then without much prompting, an arrangement was made—a simple deal of convenience. They didn't know then that this simple transaction would one day transform into something more substantial. The word friendship can't quite describe it, although it was a friendship of a sort, at times even a little more.

Together they walked up to the backpacker hotel, picked up Alice's things and on the way stopped at the beach. Soon, but still feeling disconcerted, she introduced herself formally: "Li Alice Bing-Yu; Li is my surname but you can call me Alice."

Alice Walker stayed with Li for ten days, sleeping on a couch in the studio, located on the third floor of an old building on Rue Direita Carlos Eugenio. The large window of the studio opened onto a little bay in the east. The stucco house was battered by years of rain and sun; the greenish plaster was peeling off the walls exposing patches of reddish bricks. The walls of her third floor studio and the small bedroom and kitchen at the back of it were of the colour of moist yellow ochre. There was a small terrace fenced by a stone railing, the floor cracked and covered in patches of moss and lumps of grass. In one corner of the studio was Li's small dark-room, but she processed most of her films in a more sophisticated lab, located near the soccer stadium, which she shared with two other photographers. The three large windows of her own studio were lined with blinds operated by a sophisticated mechanism to control the amount of light.

Alice enjoyed modelling for Li, needing a mere hint to grasp whatever was asked of her. Li enjoyed it as much although she didn't show it explicitly. She wanted to appear patient, unhurried, trying to make the most of the unexpected offer. They urged each other to invent and create moments of brilliance, transient and maybe that's why endearing. The camera clicked non-stop as if struggling to convert the momentary effulgence into some kind of permanence.

A few of the photos were in the style of Helmut Newton's famous *Self-Portrait with Wife and Model*. However, the model in Li's photo wasn't nude. Alice, Li knew, would have agreed to pose but she didn't feel the need to ask. The nakedness of a nude blinds the eye. It obscures things by confining the allegorical to an image. It pampers the viewer by appealing directly to his or her desire, too obvious and hence easy to satisfy. There was a time when, like any other novice, she had been obsessed with the nude, but she was glad that she had passed that phase unharmed. The world, she had come to understand, possessed many other delights that stimulated pleasure. The desire to touch, she realised, is far more intense when the object is veiled. Joy resides in the act of unveiling and not in the unveiled object itself.

The photo sessions were intense and exhausted them both. The long drives to Macau or to the island of Coloane on Li's Vespa, with Alice sitting behind holding her tight, brought both relief and fresh desire to improvise and invent.

It didn't surprise Li when Alice told her that she was a dancer in a little company in Perth. "I knew it," she explained, "the moment I saw you bend down to pick up the bowl." Their conversation had been intermittent and erratic. It wasn't that they weren't interested in knowing about each other? Rather they were fearful that any sign of urgency or desperation might undo the spell. Both found the indifference they showed each other a little bewildering. For Li, who had tested and tasted the world, it wasn't unusual, but Alice was young, just twenty-four. Where had she learned to tame the beast of curiosity, to keep the suspense suspended, to defer the moment till it shows itself?

Hence nothing was deliberately asked or divulged. In fact replies to this or that question were often delayed for hours, even days. "How old are you?" Alice asked Li once, and the reply came on the Vespa when they were driving back from the workshop of her Portuguese potter-friend. "Forty-two," Li replied. "I am twenty-four," Alice said and laughed, "You four-two and I two-four."

However, this paucity of verbal communication initiated a new and more effective mode of conversation carried out through touches. The first few attempts were hesitant and clumsy but they soon developed an intricate vocabulary of responses, instinctive and natural like any mother tongue. The body conveyed meaning without loss or exaggeration. The fear of being misunderstood or forgotten was contained. They began to feel happy with each other.

Li once saw Alice pick up a framed photo in her studio. "Yes, she is my mother," Li said pre-empting the question. What followed next surprised them both.

"There is a bit of me in her, you know," Alice said.

"I know,' Li replied, "the same way as I see a bit of me in you."

"You must be joking," Alice said.

"No, I am not," Li replied.

They both looked at the photo of Li's mother again and discovered that there definitely was a hint of likeness. Alice raised her hand to touch her face and Li explained that her remark was more like a wish that she wanted to be a bit like her. "In which way?" Alice asked.

"For instance, in the way you walk," Li replied.

The difference was rather stark. Li shuffled—short brisk steps, not hurried and yet quick, whereas Alice's was a true walk; the feet exerting the whole weight of the body and the ground under her feet responding with the same solid firmness.

Li showed Alice a print of Magritte's painting: in the sky above a city there is white cumulus and to its right a large rock with cracks and cavities, and in between them, hanging just above, a white crescent. The print had a note scribbled in quotes 'The rock doesn't fall. Why, we ask, and immediately become aware of its weight.'

"Do you always talk in riddles?" Alice had asked Li then.

After spending four weeks with Li, Alice went away to Kyoto, "to dance in the Zen gardens of Kyoto."

*

Three months after their meeting, Li wrote a letter to Alice. The letter accompanied a packet with two large A1-size black and white prints, one of which was a self-portrait with Alice.

Dear Alice,

Do you remember the rusty Vespa on which I drove you around? It has broken down and I have been told to buy a new scooter. To fix the old would be expensive, I am told.

When I mentioned the other day that there was a bit of me in you, I wasn't talking in riddles. In fact you were quite right when you noticed in my mother a hint of likeness of you.

Li Shu-Yun, my mother was born in Australia, under a

130

gum tree on a hillock near Halls Creek. The year was 1945. By the way, Shu-Yun means 'sacred cloud'. Her father, that is my grandfather, who carried the name Li Ah-Nu was a gold miner. He went to Australia in 1935 and worked in the goldfields near the town of Pine Creek, and then moved to Halls Creek to try his luck there. He worked hard but didn't find much gold. A small lead here and there, a few trinkets, but no nuggets. He soon gave up and wanted to return, but the war broke out and he couldn't find a boat to take him home.

His wife (My grandmother), he told me once, was a Gija woman. I don't remember her name. My mother too didn't know her name. When she, that is my mother, was a few months short of her first birthday, my father packed his bag and escaped to Derby to catch a boat. However, he didn't leave Derby empty handed. His little daughter was with him.

That was it; past was left behind, unspoken, unremembered, till I saw you that evening in the market with a Chinese bowl in your hand.

Like my mother, who didn't have a clue about her mother, I too don't remember anything at all about my father. He was, I understand, an Irish petty-officer on a ship who spent a week with my mother and sailed away leaving her pregnant. The clear blue eyes which you liked so much have come from him, the broad hips as well, but the soul belongs to my mother. I am quite sure about it.

My grandfather brought me up. He used to tell me stories of gold miners; how they used to fossick for gold, hunt for milky white quartz and look for creeks washing them down. He hated the heat and lack of water; and then there were crocodiles and weird reptiles. He once showed me a little canvas on which one of his friends had painted a couple of beautiful parrots.

My grandfather died a few days after my eighteenth birthday. My mother too didn't last long; in less than two years, *she too was gone.*

But the reason I am writing to you now is because I have a favour to ask. A week or so after you flew to Kyoto I started searching material about the Gija people on the web and came across a series of paintings made by a Gija man by the name of Paddy Bedford. I understand this isn't his real Gija name.

One of the paintings is unbelievably beautiful. My first reaction was to look away and I did. I turned the computer off, and went into the kitchen to cook the dinner, but I had to stop cooking and return. I turned on the computer again, and retrieved the image. It stayed on the screen for hours, glowing in the dark like an apparition. That was a mistake because slowly the colours began to seep inside me, cleaving me from inside. I felt breathless and so weak that I had to sit down for a moment. Then the phone rang. I let it ring and ring. It stopped, and relieved, I went for a walk on the beach.

I seem to have recovered now but a sense of sadness still hovers in and around me. It feels as if a hand has come to rest on my shoulder; I can't see it but the touch, I feel, is real. My friends at the photo-lab tell me that I am depressed, that I should see a doctor or a counsellor or do something different. Go on a cruise, one of them suggested, or just take a trip to Antarctica.

A few weeks ago I saw a lorikeet in my dream; very similar to the one in my grandfather's painting. I was sitting on the floor and it flew in through the window and landed in front of me. As I stretched my hand it turned into a large bird or perhaps it was me who had changed into a little thing the size of a grasshopper. Suddenly I found myself sitting on the back of the bird with my arms round its neck, and then, like a plane, it took off.

The next morning I decided that I would go to Halls Creek to see the land of my grandmother. But I am a little scared to make the journey alone, and I am wondering if you would

*have the time and patience to spend a few weeks with me on this
trip. If you are busy and if you think it would be hard for you to
come, please say no. I'll understand. But please know that your
presence would be a blessing.
I haven't heard from you since receiving your little postcard
from Kyoto and I have misgivings that my letter may not reach
you at all. But I hope it does and I hope you like the prints.
Waiting eagerly for your reply,*

Li Alice Bing-Yu

*

A month after posting the letter Li received a phone call from Alice. A
week later a large packet with two poster size prints of the two paintings
arrived. One of them was of the two women hiding on the Quartz Hill.

"Are you alright?" these were the first words spoken to her by Alice.

"Not really," she said in reply.

"Do you really want to come?"

"Of course," she said, "but I am scared."

"Of what?"

"Of myself."

"What do you mean?"

"I have never been to Australia."

"So what? It's your grandmother's home. It would be like coming
home, seeing your own country, your people."

"It isn't my country? How can it be?" And then after a pause, "Will you
come with me?"

"I'll try. I can't promise, but I'll try."

*

Thus in August that year Li landed in Kununurra to spend four weeks
walking through the country of her grandmother. She brought her camera
but took very few photos. At the airport she saw a large man waiting for

her. He was holding a sign with her name spelt properly: Li Alice Bing Yu.

"Archie Thomas," he said greeting her with a full hand-shake, "This is for you," he added handing her a note.

The brief note was from Alice in which she apologised for not being able to meet her and to be with her. She explained that she was flying off to Paris with her troupe, but had found for her the most suitable companion. Archie, she said, was one of the Gija people, the custodians of the country she was going to stay in and walk around; that he was the right person to show her the land because he knew the rules. "He is shy," she emphasised, but "loves to tell stories and in spite of his large size can dance with grace and agility. Ask him nicely and he'll show you a few steps."

Archie Thomas was a giant of a man, more than six feet tall, broad shoulders, a large round face with deep-set eyes shining in the shadows of thick eyebrows, and long dark hair with just a hint of grey. There was a deep crescent-shaped scar on his forehead, just above the right eyebrow. His voice was unusually soft, which surprised Li, more because of its whispering and at times grumbling intonations. However, most remarkable were his hands—the size of a large coconut, and like a coconut, the skin was rough and stringy.

Standing beside him Li would always feel tiny, like a little girl in a school uniform—unsure but never intimidated.

She would later find out that Archie Thomas had worked for many years as a field assistant with a company looking for diamonds in the area, where his main job was to wash and pan sand in dried-out river beds and creeks. Perhaps that is why he knew a fair bit about rocks and stones in the area.

*

Archie took Li to a small Gija community near Warmun where she spent the next four weeks seeing, watching and listening. The camera was put away so she could feel free from the imposition of a photographer's way of looking at the world. She wanted to let the world reach her, as if of its own will and desire, and flow into her. She wanted to turn herself into a river bed, to use Archie's words, that allowed every kind of detritus to stream in and settle, creating the conditions for life to seed and flourish.

However, she knew how fickle memory often is, and how easily it falls prey to the vagaries and allurements of imagination, which only need a little crack to get in, take refuge and grow into layers of encrustation. Hence, to protect herself from this inevitable onslaught of imagination, she decided to make notes in a diary. The notes were rather brief, often cryptic, here and there, illustrated with little sketches:

I can't believe how dry and desiccated the land looks. I am told in the wet season when the monsoon hits, the region transforms dramatically, but the heat of the dry season drains it out, and yet it still refuses to die.

The air is dry, the light bright, the colours blinding: red, crimson, yellow, and stretched above everything a cloudless sky. I miss the moist shades of green, the smell of the sea, the whiteness of plastered houses at home. It must be raining there now.

Last night I lay under the most glorious of skies. I have learnt to spot the Southern Cross and the Pointer. "Be patient," grandfather often told me. He'd be proud to know that I am able to locate most of the celestial birds: Grus, the crane; Pavo the peacock; Tucana, the toucan, and most fabulous of all the Phoenix. I showed Archie the starry birds and when I had finished he told me of the Emu, pointing in the sky dark lines and shapes—the head next to the Southern Cross and legs stretched along the Milky Way, touching Antares, the heart of Scorpius.

The women in the camp are very kind to me. They like the lack of curiosity I display. It isn't a deliberate ploy to please them or make them talk. I am happy to live as quietly as possible, listening and watching, and glad that I am allowed to do a few chores for them—prepare canvas boards, crush ochres for the paint, wrap up the paintings, and hand the women painters water and tea.

I am learning more and more about paints and pigments—red, yellow and white ochres. Yellow ochres contain hydroxides of iron, Archie tells me, and the white ones are made of kaolin. When heated, the yellow ochre looses water and turns brown and red. The red colour comes from a mineral called haematite derived from a Greek word haimatites, meaning 'blood-like'.

I have picked up a few words of Gija. Some sounds are hard to learn, and if the women laugh at my clumsy attempts, I laugh with them as well. The most difficult are the words which begin with 'ng', but others are easy and I like the feel of their sounds in my mouth—red ochre is called badem, and the yellow goorndoolji. When I utter goorndoolji, the round sounds of so many 'os' reminds me of the rounded shapes of the yellow lumps of ochre, and when I speak goorloom I feel and hear water gurgling down my throat. The word for a white person is gardiya. There isn't a special Gija name for the Chinese like me which disappoints me. I would have loved to learn that word.

I have brought two books to read; one of them is Ovid's Metamorphoses, which I chose for no special reason; the other is Bruce Chatwin's The Songlines, which was recommended to me by Brian, my photographer friend. Reading The Songlines I discover that Bruce Chatwin read Metamorphoses on his trip through Australia. The uncanniness of the coincidence scares me, as do the words fate and destiny. Is it possible that meeting Alice in the market that evening wasn't a coincidence? Is it possible that this trip will change me forever? Forever. Again the same silly word. I should stop using it.

I am fascinated by the way the women work on their paintings. They sing as they paint, and their songs are about the things they paint. The act of painting, I have come to understand, is more important than the painting itself. I think the purpose is to keep the stories alive. That is why they paint the same stories again and again. But with each retelling, the story alters a little; perhaps that is the reason why each painting is a little different from its predecessor.

The other day I saw the boab trees. It took me some time to call them beautiful, but beautiful they surely are. The swollen silver-grey trunk has the shape of bottles; some elegant like wine bottles, others bulbous like jars. The craggy branches protruding from the trunk look more like roots. In the wet season, large white-creamed flowers sprout from the branches, followed by luscious foliage. As the leaves fall in the dry season, large nuts hang precariously from the branches and fall easily with each waft of the wind. The most wonderful time is at night, when the grey bark of the tree glows, and the nuts rattle in the wind. It sounds like raindrops on the roof.

Yesterday I was about to put my hand in the can to retrieve lumps of white ochre and found a snake curled inside. I had to call Aunty Rita for help. She tilted the can with a stick and the snake slid out slowly and slipped into the grasses.

A few days ago Aunty Rita asked me about the photo of Bernini's Apollo and Daphne on the cover of the Penguin edition of Metamorphoses. I read her the story of Daphne turning into a tree to protect herself from Apollo's embraces. She liked the story and wanted me to read a few more.

We haven't talked about my mother or grandmother. I am shy to breach the subject, and the women too seem reluctant. I have been told that there is a place called Yarrunga or Chinaman's Garden, sixty or so kilometres north-east of Halls Creek. The Gija woman who told me of the place is Rosie. I think I should talk to her about my grandmother, because I am informed that she was born there. I am beginning to suspect that she knows the reason why I have come here.

I have seen poverty and deprivation many times in my life, but what I have witnessed on this trip is altogether different. At Warmun things are not as bad as at Kununurra, or Wyndham, where alcohol has ruined everything, but Warmun still reminds me of a refugee camp. I am appalled by the poverty. Where do these people find inspiration to paint such wonderful stories? What is the source of hope that sustains them? I don't know. It hurts even more when I see that the rest of the population in this country is so rich and prosperous, and so very proud of what it has achieved.

*

It was almost midday, and the heat was unbearable as they came out of the four-wheel drive and began to walk to the site.

The night had been unusually cold and although Li had been warned, she was hoping that it wouldn't get so hot during the day. At home in Taipa the heat was oppressive because of the humidity, but by evening the cool breeze from the sea would bring respite. Here the air fumed and the sun burned. The tracks were layered with red dust; the rocks in the creek and the red brown sandstones on the hills were too hot to touch; the patches of green along the cracks in the sandstones promised moist calm, but this was just an illusion; the glare from the white masses of clay hurt the eyes and Li wanted to keep them shut. Even the smooth bark of gums repelled because of the heat. This disappointed her, because of all the trees, she had come to like only the gums; the muted light of the evening made them look amiable, but the real change came at night when the bark glowed in the moonlight and the stringy skin rustled in the wind, and she felt as if the trees had started walking. She had experienced something similar many years ago in Russia when she spent a few nights sleeping alone in an autumn forest of birches and pines. But this made her unsettled, even fearful.

Most of the rivers and creeks were dry or filled only with tiny pools of water. Only the vegetation lining the banks reminded her that in the wet season water gushed through them. She missed the presence of water. She wanted to take off her shoes and stand and feel the fish brush and rub her feet and ankles. How soft would be the touch of moist sand, she imagined then shooed the thought away.

Rosie took her hand and they walked together. Jimmy led. His full name was Jimmy Redford but he preferred to be called Jimmy Black. Jimmy walked gingerly with a stick. Archie held his other arm and then the two stopped, waiting for the women to catch up. Jimmy had found a place to sit: a dark-green boulder, polished soft and smooth, resting in the thin shade of a red bloodwood. He sat down, took off his glasses, wiped the sweat off with his hand and put the glasses back on again. He was breathing heavily, whistling and wheezing. Archie gave him a cigarette and lit it for him. After a few puffs a smile appeared on his face. He took off his hat. The hairless scalp was dripping with sweat. He pulled a scarf out of his pocket, wiped his head and put the hat back.

Li was troubled by the heat. They found the remains of a tree trunk and she settled down. Rosie preferred the dusty ground. She squatted against the trunk. She took off her hat and fanned herself noisily. Archie remained standing, leaning against the gum when Jimmy Black began to tell the story. His crackling voice, softened by the spit issuing from his toothless mouth, was hard for Li to comprehend. After a few minutes she lost track of the story. She noticed how the wrinkled skin on his large face quivered as he spoke. It reminded her of the skin on the back of a baby elephant she had photographed years ago in a Bangkok zoo.

She already knew the story, and perhaps that is why she focused her attention on the staccato rhythm of Jimmy Black's voice as it began to grow around her like a light sheet of monsoon rain. Why rain? She asked herself? She felt breathless from the heat and thirst. She searched for something to latch onto and only then noticed the scene so familiar from the painting.

The foreground was covered by yellow and brown spinifexes, beyond which was a cluster of stooped red bloodwoods with dark stringy-barks, and scattered within them a few ghost gums—some dead, others dying; their leafless branches, stark and ruthless. The sky added softness to the scene. Lined by streaks of clouds, Li spotted a dot-like bird, flying high in the sky. An eagle, perhaps. In the field of prickly spinifexes stood dark charcoaly stumps—eleven, she counted one by one; one of them taller than the rest; its knife-like edge shining sharp. The stumps formed a circle. Inside the circle was dry, red-brown, dusty soil—criss-crossed by tracks imprinted with foot marks.

Looking west, the field gently sloped down then undulated upwards in the form of two hillocks. One of them protruded like the spine of a frilled dragon, the other was long and flat like a pinched tail. On the other side of the hill was an escarpment of red sandstone with patches of green grass and a scatter of scrubby trees. The air near the escarpment had a purplish hue, and the sunlight was bouncing off the surfaces of flaky minerals. Mica, Archie called them.

"That is the Quartz Hill," she whispered to herself, having spotted the greyish white rocks running along the spine.

After the story was finished Rosie walked with Li up to the hill. Jimmy Black and Archie remained sitting amongst the spinifexes. The two women stopped at the foot of the hillock for a moment and then climbed up, moving along the spine. It took them five to ten minutes to reach the top. They stood and turned to look at the spinifex field intruded upon by the eleven black stumps. They sat down to catch their breath. "Look," said Rosie.

Standing on the western slope of the Quartz Hill was a small tree, less than a meter and a half tall. The fissured grey bark shimmered in the light;

the tree had lost most of its leaves, but was lit up with orange-streaked yellow flowers hanging right at the edge of spindly branches. "It's a Kapok bush," Rosie told her and smiled, explaining that to see it blooming so late is next to miraculous. "You are a lucky woman," she said.

This is the hill where two Gija women hid themselves amongst the spinifexes as they watched the bodies of poor men set alight next to the site where Jimmy Black was sitting in the shade of a red bloodwood, alone, abandoned. They know the story. It remained unspoken, unheard, but real. Archie walked to the four-wheel drive, opened the door, took something out and shut the door. He turned in their direction, raised his arm and waved. There were two water bottles in his hand.

"Let's go," said Rosie. They started walking down the grey-white spine of the hillock. Li decided to turn to catch a glimpse of the miraculous Kapok. As she stepped back, she slipped and slid over the sharp rocky outcrop. She laughed to hide her embarrassment, got up on her feet and as she wiped the dust off, she noticed a cut in the middle of her right palm. The cut didn't hurt but the sight of blood streaking from the cut made her queasy. She called out for Rosie who was standing at the foot of the hillock, waiting for her.

Jimmy Black was still sitting on the rock. "I saw you slip," Archie told her. She showed him the wound. "Nothing big," she replied. Rosie washed, cleaned and bandaged the wound.

On the way back from the site, they stopped for a few hours at Yarrunga to see the remains of the shack where Rosie was born. Li was disappointed at how poor and desolate the camp looked.

Back at the community centre, Aunty Rita took off the bandage to examine the cut and told her it would require stiches to avoid a permanent scar. "I don't mind a scar," she replied then went back to her notebook.

*

Silence, her grandfather used to say, is a blessing especially when you want to listen to the whispers of your mind. It becomes a true act of benevolence when people around you understand your predicament, and leave you alone to be with yourself.

Something very similar happened to Li soon after her visit to the Quartz Hill. For several days she went into a deep recess within herself, often sitting alone with her notebook, occasionally making a note, but otherwise just sitting still and watching and listening. She was mesmerised by the choral humming of the cicadas. Like waves it rose reaching a crescendo then waned to silence, only to rise again after a two second pause. Each wave emerged from the same point in the east, traversed an arc, and finished in the bushes near the waterhole.

When her mind was not occupied with this humming she listened and talked to the voices, but slowly they began to fade, and her mind was filled with images. It felt as if her eyes had turned into the pinhole of a camera obscura, projecting visions onto the concave screen of her mind, jostling with each other to catch her attention. She, like a spoilt lover, let them play with her, refusing to bless any of them with favours. She knew that in time a sense of order would prevail, and then she would be able to unravel their mystery. As it turned out, she didn't have to wait long. The visions she discovered were mutations of the four paintings she had first seen in her studio at home. What confused her most was the way they were overlaid, juxtaposed and often sliced into by her impressions of the landscape she was now surrounded by.

That the two didn't quite match didn't disturb her. She was pleased they didn't, because a careful reproduction of the natural landscape would have disappointed her. Maybe that is the reason she was so impressed by the profound simplicity of shapes: dots, circles, straight lines and arcs. The painting as a gesture, a prompt or perhaps a concentrated residue, abstracted from the natural real.

Were colours also the residue? She didn't know. Thinking about them didn't help; it rather obstructed her seeing. Every thought she had bounced off the bright monochromes and blunted the feelings, which in a way wasn't so bad either because it helped her to escape the state of intense emotional turmoil the colours had induced. The red, white and black were, as she would have said, "easy to live with" but the impact of the blue was furious; it made her want to weep.

"Why is the blue so beautiful?" she asked.

"I don't know," she, to her great surprise, heard someone reply.

"But you painted it. Didn't you? You must know."

"I did, but without knowing."

"The soil was red, brown and yellow and there were spinifexes."

"Yes, there were."

"And yet you decided to paint them blue?"

"Yes, and painted the white Quartz Hill pitch black," she heard, followed by a crackling laughter and only then she noticed the voice.

It sounded like that of Jimmy Black, but she felt as if Paddy Bedford was speaking to her. She had seen a couple of photos of the Gija elder in an exhibition catalogue. In one of them he was holding a burnt trunk. The skin of his hands was as dark and stringy as the bark. He was wearing a blue and white check shirt, and on his head an akubra hat with sunglasses in a white frame resting on it. The face was decidedly unhappy and the eyes stared at you straight.

"Perhaps it is the smoke from the fire in the red circle?" Li asked.

"The black and blue smoke! Perhaps it is. Who knows?"

"And the smoke has turned the Quartz Hill black, the wagon tracks black, the horizon black."

Li remembered Aunty Rita telling her about the blue paint and why it was so rare in their paintings. The blue ochre was hard to find and they had to mix black and white ochres carefully to get different shades of blue; the blue, according to her, was the same as black, but with a little bit of white added to it.

"There aren't any animals or people in the painting?"

"Don't need them."

"Why? Do they distract?"

"Yes."

"So you just have circles for eyes; one for each of the two women."

"That's it. You only need to show the things that matter."

"Matter to what?"

"To the story."

"So they are all in the story: the rocks, the plants, the animals and the people; all as one in the story, and the story is the painting itself."

"Maybe."

"But there was a kapok on the hill too."

"Yes, there was, and it's a good tree, a lovely tree."

"But it isn't in the painting, I mean the story?"

"Yes, not in my story."

"Why? Would have been nice to have it."

"Maybe, but that's in your story. You paint your own kapok."

"I can't paint."

'You can if you want to ..."

She and Jimmy Black talked like this often. Brief exchanges interspersed with periods of quiescence in which images played with her mind.

The relief from the ordeal, if it was an ordeal, arrived unexpectedly. First in the form of Grace, the ten-year old grand daughter of Aunty Rita. She must have been observing her for a while because her first question to Li was: "Are you ill?"

Li replied that she wasn't ill, but sad. Grace asked her if that was the reason why she sat alone talking to herself. Li said that she didn't talk to herself, to which Grace's reply was short and emphatic: "Yes, you do."

Grace asked Li if she could look at her camera and learn how to take photos. For the first time during her trip, Li pulled the camera out of the case. They walked up to the waterhole near the camp and Li took photos of whatever Grace asked her to: termite mounds; a frilled-necked lizard sunning on the red sandstone; Grace sitting near the pool, her feet dangling in the water, holding in her hand white round pebbles; a large echidna stunned still by their sudden appearance; scribble marks on the gums, the gum nuts, and a shy rainbow bee-eater.

They were resting near the waterhole when two birds flew in and landed on the squiggly branch of a paperbark. The male, brilliant green with a scarlet shoulder patch and a splash of blue on the back; its female companion all green with just a brush of red. Grace asked her to take a photo and Li clicked and the male suddenly fell off the branch. It wasn't hurt because it soon got up and flew off followed by its friend, leaving a brassy crillik-crillik in the air.

The next day Grace gave her a boab nut on which she had carved a little fish and a frog.

In the evening, the same day, Alice arrived suddenly. "How are you sister?" she said and gave her a hug. Li told her about her trip to the site of burning near the Quartz Hill. She also told her about her short visit to the Chinaman's Garden and how defeated and distressed she felt afterwards. She didn't fail to mention the lonely kapok on the hill and how it had captured her heart.

Alice looked at the cut on her hand. "It isn't getting better," she said and they decided to go to Kununurra to have it looked at by a doctor and get a prescription for antibiotics.

*

A week later Li returned home to Taipa in the midst of a minor cyclone. It rained for three days and she found the sound of the rain on the roof soothing. During the day she kept herself busy sorting the details of a new work she had been commissioned to do. It involved photo shoots of surfers in Hawaii.

In the last week of October, a long letter from Pearl, her daughter, arrived from Edinburgh, where she was studying design. Pearl wrote that she had bought Li a return ticket to visit her during the Christmas break and that she was planning a trip to Spain and Portugal with her. She was pleased by her daughter's invitation, hoping that it would help her escape the state of anxiety she had found herself in.

But the visions of her trip to the Kimberley didn't stop invading her dreams. They were brief, haphazard and repetitive. During the day, when she had time, she re-read her notes and retraced her trip on the map on Google Earth. She enjoyed this virtual re-enactment of her journey, traversing again the imagined landscape. However, the source of the excitement wasn't so much in the re-enactment, but in the walks through the landscape of her own being, a landscape that had hitherto remained untraversed, unknown, almost alien to her.

Her fascination with the colour blue remained undiminished and she decided that on her trip back from Edinburgh she would stop in Morocco and spend some time in the little towns and villages, photographing the colour blue: the robes, the turbans, the tents and the cupolas of village mosques.

Soon after she found the most appropriate word to describe the blue in Paddy Bedford's painting with two eyes. Melancholic, she called it. It made you grieve, she said, but the grief you felt was different; no anger or hate, no clamouring for revenge or condemnation; it wanted you to forgive and look for hope; don't ask for closure, it said, but live it as an endless event of being.

With time she began to forget many particular details of her visit to the Kimberley, and of her walks in the country of her grandmother and her people. The impressions of different chores she had performed for Aunty Rita and her friends also began to fade. She was dismayed that the unforgettable moment of her first encounter with Alice in the market bending down to pick up a piece of pottery also started to slip away.

She allowed these moments to wilt because she wanted to keep the memory of one particular moment alive forever; the moment when she had slipped and hurt her hand trying to catch the very last glimpse of the lonely kapok blooming on the slope of the Quartz Hill.

But because she doubted her will to keep the trace of even that encounter alive, a few days after returning from her trip to Morocco she went to a friend at the local nursery and asked her to get her a small kapok from the Kimberley. The friend appeared bemused by her request but assured her that she would do her best to find the plant for her.

It took nine weeks for the plant to arrive. Li bought a large pot filled with soil similar to the one in the country of her grandmother and planted the kapok. The pot was placed on the terrace outside her window. Her friend warned her that the plant might not survive the humidity and salty sea air of Taipa, but Li was confident that she would do her utmost to make the kapok feel at home.

Faust Cantata: Unreliable Notes for an Autobiography

I open my eyes. The room is dark and in the darkness I see Ira sitting in a chair. She is asleep. I open my mouth to speak but the darkness spreads over me and I drown under the silky sheet, wet and warm like the sea.

The next time I open my eyes the room is so bright that it hurts my eyes. I want to shield them. I try to lift my arm and hand but the effort exhausts me. I moan and Ira notices that I am awake and I begin to hear her speak. Although I can recognise her voice I am unable to grasp the words. They are coming out, as if from a well trailed by echoes; each word swallowed by the echo walking behind.

These moments of awakening are brief, the length of a short breath. Like a stone dropped in a lake they only ripple the surface of the dream-laden sleep. I dream non-stop. So continuous is their presence that I sometimes feel, if one can feel and think while asleep and dreaming, that when I finally regain consciousness I'll fail to recognise if I am no longer asleep, no longer dreaming.

Most dreams I see are moments of stillness, what the painters describe as *nature-morte*, still nature, waiting to be touched by a hand or a look, and come to life. And I am glad that they are still. I hate the tyranny of stories; the imposition that all forms of art have to tell a story, that what matters most is the passage of time, that unless we can thread the moments together their wholeness will disintegrate like beads fallen off a necklace. Why do we think that we need to arrange the moments into a sequence in order to keep them safe in memory? Why? The nascent purity of a moment, I am more than certain, can be preserved by the moment itself.

Here is one: Ira stands in front of the mirror, her right hand touching the necklace. From the sofa I see her fully; her face in the mirror and her back, which she can't see herself. That's the moment—the necklace around her beautiful neck. The rest is immaterial, insignificant.

Sometimes moments appear juxtaposed, a montage of no particular sequence, as if ejaculated by the subconscious in spills and spurts. I let them come and go; their mere presence indulges me. They please me; not as the thought of a feeling would have pleased, but as the feeling itself; like a sip of the lukewarm milk that Grandma used to leave for me each morning in a glass jug on the table.

However, it would be dishonest to suggest that I don't want some of these spurts to linger a little longer. I want to hang onto this or that moment, for no particular reason, just because some of them tickle me inside. I want to grab the metaphorical hand, stretched in my direction, hold a finger and walk. That's when I make a mistake: in my eagerness to walk with them I begin to order them. I have fallen prey to the charm of a clever storyteller. "Go away you cunning clown," I reprimand, but after a pause, I give in.

There I am, standing on the cobbled Singerstraße. The day is bright, the street empty and I stand immobilised with my school bag stuck on my back unable to decide if I should go to school or not. The day is so unusually wonderful.

.... It's late in the night and I am awake in bed. The window is open. The curtains wave in the breeze and I hear someone walking in the street with a horse. I get up to check and am disappointed that the horse isn't white.

.... The bells are ringing and, unable to wait for my brother Viktor who is terribly slow, I rush to reach St. Stephens Cathedral and float in the voluminous waves of sounds. But Viktor trips, falls and cries and I have to return to help him up. The moment of surfing on the sounds of bells remains lodged in the closet I call hope. Hope, what a decent word it is. Decent and sweet.

.... This one is rather special. It announces its presence emphatically and I hear the words '12th December 1977, 6 pm' read aloud as if by a voice-over in a film. The lift doesn't work and I run up the stairs and reach the door on the fifth floor. I do it instinctively without a shred of doubt. I knock. Once, twice, then push the door and see her sitting at the piano. She turns and looks and I look at myself through her eyes, as if it was her point-of-view shot, and find that I am a twelve-year old boy in a school uniform with a Pioneer's tie. She points at the stool beside her and I go and sit and we play together something by Schubert. Only then I realise that I have come to invite Frau Charlotte Ruber to the performance of my *Concerto Grosso*. She declines, saying she isn't feeling well, and as I walk back onto Singerstraße, I am caught in cold drizzle. A black dog runs past, stops at the sandstone column, sniffs and begins to piss.

The dream ends. I wake up.

"Where is the black dog?" I ask. Ira mutters something.

"The black dog?" I ask again. She looks at me surprised and speaks again but I can't make any sense of what she says, and I am unable to understand why.

On Sunday at five past five in the morning I come out of my coma. Six weeks pass before I start speaking Russian again. That also happens on a Sunday: *Voskreseniye*, as we say in Russian; sounds like *Voskresheniye* (resurrection).

*

I am fifteen. In a couple of months I'll turn sixteen. Last year Uncle Anatoly found a dacha for us, which we rent from an awful man who we have named Ostap Bender because he is cunning and heartless like the real Ostap Bender in *The Twelve Chairs*.

The wooden house is falling apart. The rooms are always damp and cold. Last winter there was hoarfrost in the corners of the room. The house has two rooms divided by a wall that doesn't reach the ceiling. My brother Viktor, sister Irina and I sleep in one room. Papa and Mama sleep in the other. At night I often hear them arguing. I know things aren't good but they are far better than they used to be in Moscow where we spent the last year moving from place to place. There were days when Irina had to sleep in Grandma Thea's small room and Viktor and I stayed either with Grandpa Viktor or with our parents.

At least now we are together.

The village is called Valentinovka. It isn't far from Moscow. Just an

149

hour or so by train. Papa goes to work in Moscow. Like Grandma Thea he translates and edits articles for a weekly magazine in German.

I too go daily to Moscow, often with Papa. I have started attending the October Revolution College of Music. It is well known for its choir and folk music. I have joined the Choirmaster's Department. I like it there. "I want to be a composer," I tell Mama, who just laughs, which annoys me. She likes listening to Strauss's waltzes, and Tchaikovsky's *Swan Lake* is her favourite, but she neither understands nor wants to understand how music is made. Papa on the other hand takes music more seriously. He loves Shostakovich's *Seventh Symphony*, which he once heard performed during the war. The war has ended but he still can't stop talking about the symphony. When he is at home working, the radio plays music in the background, and sitting in my room I hear them both, his typewriter and the music on the radio.

A few years ago he tried to get me interested in science and mathematics and was disappointed that I was more keen on music and literature. I hope he doesn't regret buying me my first accordion. He appears to have accepted my decision and seems pleased that I haven't changed my mind. "He is very determined you know," I have often heard him telling Mama about me. But Mama is convinced that I have made a grave mistake. I understand her doubts. She wants me to have a proper degree that will lead me to a decent job. She'll change, I am sure, she will. She is the one who convinced Papa to get a piano for me to practice at home. The piano sits in the room I share with Viktor and Irina. It must be annoying for them to hear me practice non-stop. For them it is nothing but noise, at least the way I play. But they both know how madly I am in love with music and because they love me they are ready to put up with my eccentricities.

We don't have a laundry in the house, and it is my duty each week to take the dirty washing to Moscow, get it washed, and bring it back. I hate the chore, mostly because often I have to wait for hours for it to dry, and travelling alone in a late evening train isn't fun. However, on laundry day I also get a chance to spend some time with Grandma Thea, who likes to talk about music, new books and films.

In the train coming home I often see two boys of my age. One of them is unusually big and strong. The other is rather short and thin and has a sickly appearance. Their presence makes me uncomfortable. As soon as I see them I normally change my seat or move to another coach. Luckily they don't follow me, but they have tried to bully me once or twice. On one occasion, finding me alone in the coach, they came and sat down on either side of me. The big boy then stood up in front of me and shouted "Dirty *Zhid* (Jew)". I didn't respond and waited for their next move but then a young militiaman entered the coach and the boys left me alone.

Being called a *Zhid* didn't surprise or hurt me. What hurt me more was the fear I felt in their presence. To be sneered at like this isn't new to me. It has happened before, but only they, the two odd boys, were able to scare me. I once asked Viktor if he too was harassed or bullied. "Never," was his reply. So there must be something wrong with me. I think it's my face. To hide it is impossible, so why should I fret about it? Why? In fact I should be glad that we are Jewish. It saved us from being exiled to Siberia. At least that's what my Papa believes. During the war, the authorities were ready to deport us because we spoke German, but Papa was able to convince them that his parents were Jews from a little village in Latvia. We were spared.

Two days ago Papa gave me a new German book to read. It is *Doctor Faustus: The Life of the German Composer Adrian Leverkuhn* by Thomas Mann.

To read a book about a German composer, his life and music, is very exciting. Papa has a good collection of books in German: Heine, Goethe, Hölderlin, Hesse, and even Novalis. Both he and Mama encourage me to read them. The first few pages are always difficult but after I grasp the rhythm and pace of writing, the reading becomes easy. We often speak German at home, which also helps. I find conversing with Papa hard. His German sounds more correct and bookish. Mama on the other hand prefers a more colloquial version and speaks with a Russian accent. With her I can speak without thinking, almost instinctively.

A year or so ago I found on Papa's shelf an old edition of Johann

Spies's sixteenth-century *Volksbuch* about Dr. Johann Fausten. The book was published in Frankfurt and it appears papa must have bought the book in Frankfurt, the place where he was born.

I enjoyed reading the *Volksbuch*, but Mann's book is rather big and not an easy read. In spite of this I am going to persevere, especially with the sections where the compositions of Adrian Leverkuhn are described in great detail. I find music-making very mysterious and the thought that I am going to experience the mystery, feel and enjoy it, excites me. I feel privileged.

*

"Andryusha," I call him. He is watching something on the television.

"Listen Andryusha," I call again and although I know he doesn't want to hear anything I am saying, I continue. "When you were tiny, I mean very tiny ..." (and I show with my hands how tiny he was), "your Mama and I used to put a bath tub on two chairs and wash you. You used to scream your heart out, enraging your Grandpa who would be watching ice hockey on the television in the same room."

Andrei ignores me but I don't want to give up, and continue. "Do you remember Pitsunda? I took this photo there." I want to show him the photo, which I saw in the album the other day. He was six then. Very good-looking, a bit girlish. He is wearing a striped T-shirt painted with black and white horses. He is holding a little monkey in his arms. The monkey appears happy, grasping Andrei's left arm. I look at Andrei's hands. How big they are. Long delicate fingers. From his mother, I am sure. "You had a little monkey ..."

"Yes, Misha." He gets off the chair, kicks it aside and walks into his room slamming the door shut. Both Ira and I know what will happen next. He'll pick up his electric guitar; turn up the volume and play. Shrill angry sounds. Rage. I am unable to understand why he is so angry. Maybe he is angry with me?

He must think I don't love him or don't love him enough. I love him. How can it be otherwise? I know that I am clumsy the way I do it but I do love him. It is also true that lately I have been very busy, but if I say no to the commissions they'll soon stop coming and it won't be easy to win them back.

I also concede that I like talking about music. It doesn't matter if my interlocutors are friends or strangers. They phone me and often knock on our door without invitation or appointment. But I can't hang up the phone on them or tell them to go away. They look and sound keen and earnest and I lack the courage to say no. And then there are my students. They surely need my help, especially when they are so nice to me. The students need encouragement, even those with little or no talent. In fact the ones with little talent need it even more. With time they'll themselves realise that they should do something else, but one can only drop a hint without breaking their hearts, unlike my not-too-diplomatic teacher, who told me point blank that I should give up the piano for good. "Your right-hand fingering is shoddy," he declared. I knew that myself, and I also knew the reason behind this unfortunate development. But I didn't want to blame the accordion for ruining my hand and fingering. I loved my accordion. Dear Frau Ruber noticed the defect immediately. She, and the accordion convinced me that I should learn to become a composer and not a pianist.

I remember Papa taking a photo of me with my first accordion. It was in Vienna. I saw the accordion and decided that I needed it immediately. I went back to our apartment, pulled out my collection of rare stamps and sold it to buy the beautiful instrument. I felt bad selling the collection but I didn't have anything else of value. That accordion is still with me and I do occasionally play it, but as I look at my face in the photo I spot a marked resemblance to Andrei, especially the eyes. This should not surprise me, but it does. However, what distresses me more is the thought that he has also inherited some of my other ailments.

Both my grandmother and mother had bad hearts and both of them died from strokes. My sister Irina suffers from the same ailment and Viktor has already been warned. My kidneys don't function properly and I have endured recurring migraines my whole life. I have learnt to live with these disorders and so should Andrei. "Don't be stupid," Ira scolds me. I agree.

Andrei is just seventeen. It must be very hard for him to know that his heart can capitulate any day. I have this niggling suspicion that he blames me for this predicament. "Is that right?" I often ask Ira. "Yes and no," she always replies. Yes, because the bad heart has definitely come from me and my side of the family. No, because she is sure Andrei isn't such an idiot to blame me. The firmness with which she voices her opinion should reassure me but somehow it doesn't and I am overcome by despair.

I still remember the day when he fell ill and the doctors diagnosed the illness. "It can't be treated fully but it can be controlled," the doctors told us. I didn't know what to do or say.

I had been working terribly hard that year trying to meet tight deadlines. Just a week earlier I had finished the score for a feature film based on Pushkin's *Little Tragedies*, and was quite pleased with the effort. I suppose I could have given him more time but there wasn't any to spare. He must have felt neglected, abandoned. But Ira didn't say anything. She should have warned me. Perhaps she did and I just ignored her.

The diagnosis stunned us. We were advised to change our lifestyle. To work less, to find more time for Andrei and to ask him to slow down as well. It was hard. Andrei refused to listen. Stubborn, like his mother. "I'll either live like everyone else or not live at all," he declared. Rage followed. That's what happens when one loses hope. "Why me? Why now?" I am sure he must have asked. And in a rage he started doing things he shouldn't have. I felt miserable for not being able to help him.

Soon he joined a rock-group, started his own band and began staying out at night. There were drugs going around. We were scared. Even Ira, my saviour, looked confused and nervous. At home, he would lock himself in his room and rehearse. It was terrible. I decided then to learn more about rock music, to see how it works and thereby find a way to reach him.

He noticed my efforts and it definitely made him happy, but the relief was temporary. A year and a half later we observed a sudden change in Andrei and although it lasted only a few weeks, a ray of hope appeared. This happened after he had spent three nights out with his friends. We didn't know where he had gone. We just saw a brief note on the dining table saying that he was going away. Ira phoned his friends but failed to get any information. He returned on Thursday. It was quite late at night. I was still working. Ira had gone to bed. She came out as soon as she heard his voice. Andrei came in and sat with me at the table, looked at what I was doing, and gave me a hug. He saw Ira standing at the door and went up to her, smiled and hugged and kissed her. He said he was hungry and Ira warmed some soup for him. He ate sitting at the table making small talk, which was quite unusual. He finished the soup and asked if there was some ice-cream for him.

A few days passed without incident. One night, unable to make any sense of the change, I decided to ask Ira.

"Irochka," I said, "is Andryusha alright?"

"What do you think?" she answered. She was lying on the bed, her faced turned to the window.

"So you don't know?"

She turned round and looked straight at me and said, "I know."

"And ..."

"He has got himself a girl friend."

"A girl friend?"

"Did he tell you?"

"No, but I can smell her. She is all over him, his clothes, his hair ..."

"But he is just a kid."

"He is eighteen, stupid. Not a kid any more."

A few months later we met Agnessa, his girl friend. I liked her. Ira even more.

*

Early this year I read Kafka's *In der Strafkolonie*. I think it is his best story, far better than *The Metamorphosis*. The story is about a prison officer who is put in-charge of a new machine called the *Harrow*. He likes the machine because it isn't designed merely to torture a prisoner. Its main function is to inscribe messages on the prisoner's body. The machine is fitted with a unique contraption studded with nails and pins. The prisoner is stripped naked and tied to a flat platform onto which the contraption is slowly lowered. Specially designed stencils are inserted into the machine to inscribe messages such as, 'Don't Steal', 'Don't Kill', 'To Sin is Bad'. These messages are engraved first on the back, and then on the front, and after twelve-hours of slow torture, the dead body of the condemned is thrown into a ditch under the machine.

The story takes a Kafkaesque turn when the officer undresses himself and lies down on the machine to get the words 'Be Just' tattooed on his body. The act is witnessed by one of the prison inspectors, who is both bemused and horrified by the spectacle. A prison guard and a condemned prisoner assist the officer to go through the ordeal, which ends when the prison officer is dead.

I was shocked by the story, although it made me laugh too. The idea of writing a symphonic piece based on it came a week later. I usually work very fast and the piece was ready in a few weeks. It surprised me. It will be performed in October this year at the *Donaueschingen Festival of New Music*. The director of the festival wants me to provide a short statement about the piece for the program. In my statement I explain that my main intention is to explore how different versions of the same musical idea can be conjoined into a single composition. I mention that the piece deploys a serial structure, which is revealed just after the final octave. The fuzzy cluster of tones with which the piece begins, expands and rarefies, changing into successively wider intervals, which slowly become repetitive, like the punching of a stencil by an automatic machine. In order to explain the twelve-tone series which forms the basic structure, I draw attention to Kafka's *In der Strafkolonie* in which the prisoners are slowly tortured for twelve hours before they are killed. I am asked to tell a little more about the story and suddenly notice that I have somehow overlooked the shock and horror I had felt reading the story, and so have betrayed the story and my own emotional response to it. All of a sudden the music begins to sound bland and mechanical. It is undoubtedly clever, and although I am pleased by its technical accomplishment, I am disturbed by my inability to express the tragedy of Kafka's story.

Ira tells me not to worry about it, although she doesn't fail to remind me that on the day I finished the piece, the Red Army and its allies had invaded Kafka's Prague.

Strangely, I find solace in Adrian Leverkuhn's suggestion that music need not be composed slavishly to serve an idea or emotion. It should rather explore the formal structure of musical sounds.

I have been reading and re-reading Mann's *Doctor Faustus* this year. This is my third reading of the book. The first time I read the book I was just fifteen. Ten years later, the book seemed more accessible. However, even then my desire to focus on the fictional musical compositions was compromised by the story, especially the extreme anguish with which the narrator describes the tragic fate of Germany, caught in the throes of two lost wars and a brutal dictatorship. As I write this I recognise that we too have endured the same agony, assuaged to some extent by the euphoria of the final victory that promised hope. In a way our story is even more tragic, because unlike the Germans we haven't tasted freedom. Our life is ruled by apathy and pessimism. We have learned to live in silence. It's easier that way.

Is this the reason I shun politics of any kind? Unfortunately, yes. I have taught myself to keep low and out of sight. To make a martyr out of me isn't possible. I don't possess the resilience of Shostakovich or Prokofiev, and I have no desire to suffer like them. I just want to write music, teach if I can, and live a peaceful life without putting someone else's life in danger.

And I am no Mozart or Beethoven. I am a plodder, just like my beloved Bach, who was truly blessed by God. Bach is the centre of gravity of my musical world. Like the sun, he bestows light and warmth on whatever I see, dream, and happen to write. The rapturous in him overwhelms me and I often feel vanquished, uncertain that I will ever be able to write something even half as joyful. There is joy that makes you want to stand near an open window and shout and to let the people know that you are happy, and that by sharing the moment you hope to gladden their hearts. But the joy that emanates from Bach is different. Like whispers of a loving mother, it assures you about your life in the world; it assures you that while you are asleep, benevolent God will watch over you and over the world, so that when you get up in the morning it won't have turned into a nightmare.

I clearly remember the moment when I first saw little Andryusha in the crib. I was holding him wrapped tightly in a blanket in my arms. I wanted to kiss him, but was scared that I might hurt him. "Go on, kiss him," Ira said, and I did. He opened his eyes, yawned and went back to sleep. A divine miracle. No music can ever express the joy I felt then. Joy mixed with awe and bewilderment.

I suppose that is why I write music like a plodder, quite aware of my limitations. I don't require Stravinsky's absolute silence to work. I am happy in my small room with the radio or the television turned on. The noises from the street stream in; the telephone rings, the kids run up and down the street. Nothing disturbs me. I just write and write; incessantly, according to Ira; yes, she is right; I seem to write even in my sleep. If in the process something extraordinary happens I accept it with humility and move on.

*

Larissa is dead. I can't believe it but she is definitely dead, killed in a car crash. She and four other members of the crew working on the location of her new film. I can't imagine the state in which Elem must be. He must blame himself for not looking after her, for letting her go. But to keep Larissa tied down was impossible. He knew that. We all knew that. She married him on the condition that he wouldn't interfere with her work. He didn't.

It's good that she didn't ask me to write music for the film she was shooting. Good, because if Elem in the future decides to complete the film, it would be very hard to ignore Larissa's tragic death.

I met her through a friend in the Mosfilm studio. That year, (and the year was 1971), I broke my own record. Eight films with my scores were released that year. Larissa liked what I had done for *Uncle Vanya*. I liked it too.

At Mosfilm they like working with me. I am not fussy or precious about my music. I just write, and most of the times leave it to the directors to choose whatever they find useful. The unused bits are never wasted. They reappear in my other compositions. I like the process. For me it works like a lab in which I experiment. I write, it is played, and if I don't like it, I change it the very same moment. If I sound like a bricklayer, so be it, because that's how I sharpen my technique, learn to work fast and effectively, the way Anton Chekhov used to write his stories for Suvorin's newspaper.

Larissa asked me to write music for her next feature film. *You and Me* was released in 1972. I did it because she had asked. I'll have to confess that I wasn't particularly inspired by the story and the film, and had surmised that she wouldn't ask me again. But she did and I am glad that she did, because working on her next film made me proud. The music also turned out well. I am satisfied with the score and the way Larissa has used it in the film.

I know the story. Larissa also gave me the script to read and invited me to see the unedited reels. I was stunned by the film. I didn't ask her why her Sotnikov, a Russian partisan tortured and then hanged by the Nazis, looked like a Russian Jesus. There was no need. It felt natural. Seeing the reels stirred something deep inside me.

That I am a believer isn't new to me and if this is one of the reasons I find a home in Bach, that doesn't surprise me either. It feels as though I have always been a believer. Perhaps the seeds were planted in Vienna where I used to spend so much time in churches. Music was just an excuse. No, not an excuse, but a catalyst and a gift.

I am sure Ira knows about it. I haven't talked to her but there is no need. She knows me better than I do. Nothing remains hidden from her.

Larissa asked me about the score for the film and how I wished it to be used. She wanted to find out if there was something special I had intended to express. The word that came at once to my mind then was 'internal'; that whatever I had written was meant to come out of Sotnikov, from his innermost being. It wasn't meant to represent the plot or the harsh snow-laden landscape, but the intonations of his delicate, sensitive and invincible spirit. I explained to her that I had resisted using tonal clusters of heightened dissonance, but chosen instead strings playing in muted harmony. In the sequence showing the hanging of Sotnikov and three other villagers, one of whom is a twelve-year old girl, I added elements of an orchestral echo to create the illusion of an endless, almost multi-dimensional, space.

Larissa understood my intentions immediately and used the score accurately and honestly. She stitched the music to a series of close-up shots of Sotnikov. It felt as if we were lying down with him on the cold snow, gazing at the light streaks of clouds, seeing the world as he was seeing it, and making his inner music our own.

The only moment that intrigued me a little was right in the finale when the music followed Rybak, the other partisan who, in order to save his life, agreed to collaborate with the brigade of Russian policemen recruited by the Nazis. His attempts to hang himself in a latrine of the camp fail, and as he steps out to make way for another desperate policeman, he sees in front of him the snow-covered mounds littered here and there with leafless birches and pines, and the music begins to sound—the same music which Sotnikov had heard earlier in the film. It took me a while to understand the meaning of this uncanny juxtaposition. I didn't ask Larissa to explain but waited for the moment to unravel itself. The music celebrated the humanity of Rybak. Of course he is weak, pathetic and selfish, but who isn't? People like Sotnikov are rare. To measure up to them is humanly impossible. Don't love Rybak, if you so wish, but you haven't any right to hate him. He has sinned because he is human like us, weak and fallible.

Now dear Larissa too has gone. I have noted the date: 19 June 1979. I won't forget it; not only because she was a dear friend but also because her tragic death has made me think once again about her wonderful film and the minor role I have played in its making.

Her death has made me think about my own life, the music I write and the reason I write.

I have finally decided to make it public that I believe in God and that I want to be formally initiated.

*

I am in Vienna. This is my third visit. The one in 1978 had been rather brief and I had spent the whole week or so in a state of exaltation. I had been shaken by the encounter and since then the impressions of the short stay have found a permanent home in my dreams.

Two years later when I was leaving for Vienna, Viktor, my younger brother, said something rather strange. He wanted me to stand in front of the apartment on Singerstraße and imagine that he was with me. However, when I asked him what exactly he missed about Vienna he was unable to name anything. The incongruous nature of his longing, if it was longing, amazed me because for me the place is as real as any street in Moscow, and not only because it is the city where Frau Ruber lives.

I did what he had asked and phoned him that evening. The line was bad but I told him that I was planning to visit Frau Ruber. "You are a lucky man," I remember him saying.

I am indeed lucky.

I went to see Frau Ruber the following evening. I wanted to invite her to one of my lectures at the Hochschule für Musik where I was going to discuss my *Sonata for Violoncello and Piano*. She was kind and friendly but looked unusually frail. She was thinner and paler and had shrunk quite a bit. The stoop with which she walked frightened and saddened me. I couldn't stop thinking that I might not see her again on my next visit. That the same thought worried her as well became clear to me as I was about to take leave. She walked up to the old dear piano and picked up a sheet carefully tucked inside a plastic sleeve. She gave me the sheet, shook my hand and said goodbye.

Only in my hotel room that night did I notice that it was a page of Mahler's manuscript of an unfinished sketch for a piano quartet. I phoned Ira immediately to let her know about the gift. She wasn't alone and wanted me to call again the day after. "Guests," she said, before I got a chance and I had to hang up. Before hanging up, she asked me if I was feeling alright. "A bit nervous," I wanted to say, but didn't, deciding that

I'd give her a full report of the event the next day.

The events of the following day kept me busy and I wasn't able to talk to her for a few days. She meanwhile called and left a brief message at the reception.

The ceremony took place at 9.30 in the morning. I had decided to go through it on my own. I could have asked Frau Ruber to come but somehow I couldn't. I think it was wise not to ask. Ira would have definitely come with me. I am not sure about Andryusha. I would have very much liked him to be present, but I was also scared that his cynicism might stain the sanctity of the occasion.

In a way it was most appropriate that I was alone; it's a strictly personal matter, I bear the sole responsibility for the consequences, and although I realise that I may have offended people, I was ready to live with that offence. What mattered most to me was to be true to the voice I heard within me.

I am not sure why I selected that particular church. St. Stephens Cathedral seemed too grand, so was the *Votivkirche*, with its tall spires and marble stones. This *Augustinekirche* stands almost unnoticed behind the imposing shape of the Albertina Gallery. Its single tall spire hides more than it shows, and that's what I liked most. When I stepped inside, the beauty of the white Gothic interior becalmed me. The state of acquiescence it imposes seemed wished for, and when the choir sang, accompanied by the organ emitting dense volumes of sounds, the world came alive; so serene and joyous, that it made me feel both humble and proud to exist in this world in spite of its brutal ugliness.

I liked the presence of the black robed monks who I occasionally saw in the church. The fact that the church has hosted a cloister for Augustinian friars uplifted my heart even more. It was the connection with St. Augustine I cherished most. The sense of medieval piety and devotion, its discipline and rigour for sacrifices, however small, filled me with joy.

Heinrich Lundberg, a dear friend, performed the initiation. He was surprised I didn't want any music or singing. At first I had thought of asking my friends at the Hochschule für Musik to perform *Agnus Dei* from Bruckner's *Mass in F Minor*, but I decided that it would appear too pretentious. I didn't need music. I hear it all the time. My mind and heart overflow with it. After the ceremony I mentioned to Heinrich that I had asked Father Nikolai Vedernikov, an Orthodox priest in Moscow, for guidance, and that every six months I was going to invite him to my house to hear my confession.

I had become a Catholic. A German Jew born and bred in Russia had converted. It was a miracle that had to happen, and that it occurred in Vienna, my spiritual home, pleased me even more.

I phoned Ira late in the evening and told her about the ceremony in *Augustinekirche*. I mentioned that it's a small but very beautiful church, and that many years ago Schubert conducted his *Mass in F Minor* there. I told her that I had decided to start work on my *Faust Cantata*.

I asked her about Andrei and she told me not to worry about him, that he was fine. She was pleased that he and his girlfriend had agreed to accompany her to hear Rakhmaninov's *The Bells* in the concert hall of the Moscow Philharmonic. She warned me not to work too hard fearing that it would trigger a bad migraine. I asked her to remind Andrei that I needed his help with the cantata, to tell him that I loved working with him, and that his expertise in rock music was going to be very useful.

That I resolved to start work on the cantata, in Vienna, wasn't a mere coincidence. Nothing ever was. At least not for me. I am sure my visit to Frau Ruber played a part. To say that I wanted to write the cantata for her isn't correct, but that I wanted her to be present when it was performed is true.

That I had been reading Mann's *Doctor Faustus* was significant too. I read how Mann's Leverkuhn decided to rent a room in a house in the little town of Waldshut. He stayed for almost twenty years in that Abbot's chamber composing music which included the famous *Lamentation of Dr Faustus*. The Abbot's chamber got its name because it had served as a study to the head of the order of Augustinian monks, the same order for which a few cloisters were built in the *Augustinekirche* where I received my initiation.

A mere coincidence, I laughed, but to have dismissed it so lightly wasn't wise, for there is truly something magical about the story. Magical and melancholic. It was whispering inside me, asking to be set free. I made it wait but the time had come when I needed to let it become music.

*

My friends say I suffer from hypochondria. I agree, but I also suffer from real ailments, which really hurt. The migraines aren't imaginary. That at times it's hard for me to piss normally isn't imaginary either. Ira laughs when I tell her I feel jealous hearing someone urinating in the public lavatory with gusto, the stream rushing out untrammelled. I carry a bag full of medicines with me. I have got used to them like the puffer, which my dear friend Aleksei keeps with him all the time. He suffers from asthma, and had to give up singing. Now he writes reviews. Fortunately they are very good—incisive and helpful.

The other day he mentioned that I remind him of Mann's Adrian Leverkuhn. It was funny he should say that. Ira had mentioned it a number of times, too, and I agree that there is a lot of Leverkuhn in me. At times, I too have felt depressed at times, out of place, and worthless. But luckily I had Ira, Andrei and friends like Aleksei to support me.

Aleksei has somehow guessed that the reason I am reading Mann's *Doctor Faustus* is that I want to turn the fictional composition of a fictional hero into a real piece of music. I remember him telling me once about Anna, Fyodor Dostoevsky's wife, and how the two had travelled to Basel to see Holbein's famous *The Body of the Dead Christ in the Tomb*. As he described those events as reported in Anna's diary, Aleksei confessed that like Anna, he too was excited by the thought that one day he might hear one of Leverkuhn's compositions brought to life by me. "Which one?' I had dared to ask him then. "*The Apocalypse*," he had replied.

I told Aleksei that *The Apocalypse* was rather tedious, but that I had finished a cantata quite similar in structure to Leverkuhn's *Lamentation of Dr. Faustus*, and that like the lamentation, it is also based on Johann Spies's popular text. I showed him the music and played him the tango-movement.

The *Faust Cantata* was performed in June 1983 at the Vienna Festival, and although I had wished Frau Ruber to be present at the performance, she couldn't make it due to ill-health. It has since then been performed in the Tchaikovsky Concert Hall in Moscow. Unfortunately the Moscow performance was turned into a farce. Both Andrei and I agree that it was a mistake to invite Alla Pugacheva, the Soviet pop star, to sing the song of Mephistopheles. She was too famous for the role and a five-minute tango was too little for her larger-than-life persona. No wonder she went on and on.

In a way I am glad that the cantata is finished and I have washed Mann and his Leverkuhn out of my system. I feel free and ready to work on new things. But this freedom has come at a price. It is true that I have written quite a few new pieces, and some of them have been duly praised, especially the score for the film the *Feast in Time of Plague*. But to me they feel uninspired, technically superb, but ordinary. Has the spark gone? I often wonder, particularly when critics, especially my friends, keep on reminding me that the *Faust Cantata* is by far the best thing I have ever written. They don't realise how disheartening this comment is. I am only fifty, too young, I hope, to stop dreaming. That I have reached my peak from which, after a short respite I will slowly descend into mediocrity, depresses me. The performance of my little ballet at the Bolshoi and the shouts of 'bravo' after the performance didn't please me. I had to walk onto the stage, take a bow and accept the audience's adulations. Since then the word has spread that I have been accepted and acknowledged by the establishment.

However, life isn't totally bleak, and I should thank my good fortune that I have managed to keep out of trouble. Andryusha is looking better. The signs of depression have passed. The marriage has helped. Agnessa's presence has brought joy and both Ira and I are excited by the prospect of welcoming a grandchild. We need a baby in this house. In fact I am convinced that we ourselves should have tried to have another child, a little brother or sister to Andrei. "It would be hard to manage, dear Alfi," Ira used to say often, and she was right. Looking after Andrei wasn't easy. Ira had to do everything. I was too busy with my work and too incompetent to help her.

But thank God, Andrei is happy now. He likes the recording studio we have built for him in the apartment. The work too has started coming. He says that he enjoys making music for films, which is good, because it helps me as well. He accepts my congratulations, and although I praise him only because I find his music inspired, he is irritated that without my contacts it wouldn't be easy for him to get commissions. He is right. I too would have felt the same in his position, but he shouldn't be so naïve. He should just use these opportunities to make a place for himself. "Talent alone," I tell him often, "isn't enough."

The summer this year is unusually hot. Soon the International Film Festival will be over and we'll pack up and fly off to Pitsunda. Liana Iskadze, my talented student, writes that the weather is wonderful, and that she has procured for us a large stock of delicious Georgian wine. I like Pitsunda. The beach is lovely, the sun warm and friendly, and people talk more freely. The distance helps. "Out of sight out of mind," that's what people say. I think Chekhov was quite right when he said that the warm climate of the tropics makes people graceful, soft and forgiving. Is this because he met a local woman in Ceylon and fell in love with her? He should have stayed there a little longer, to let his ailing lungs recover a little. He didn't. Some say he couldn't because like many gifted Russians he was doomed and destined to die young.

We are doomed as well, although they say a ray of light has suddenly appeared. The whispers have emerged that a more benevolent ruler has arrived. His name is Mikhail Gorbachev. He is young and the insiders who know something about his life and that of his family, believe or perhaps hope that he will be kind to his people. I hope he is.

*

The ordeal is over. I have survived. The autumn has all but gone, although there are days when for a few hours the sun floods the room with soft light of vibrant colours. It feels good to be alive.

I was in a coma, and three times the doctors had pronounced me dead, ready to turn off the switch. Ira didn't let them.

166

Ira, my angel, is bringing me back to life, helping me to recover my bearings in the lost world of memories. I tell her that my past seems more like a dream, so close and yet distant, removed and alien. That it was lived by me once upon a time surprises me. But she laughs it off. Her intention is to keep telling me stories, as if I am her little Andrei. I enjoy her tales and, like Andrei, believe them to be true, because I also believe that she still loves me.

In the last week of June, I am told, we went to Pitsunda to stay at the resort. Liana Iskadze had invited us to participate in the music festival where she was going to play my music. She had asked Gennady Rozhdestvensky to conduct the *Concerto Grosso No. 1*, which was a real surprise. Andrei came with us. He likes Pitsunda, and we had hoped that the sea and the beach would lift his spirits, but he was missing Agnessa, who, for some reason or other, couldn't accompany us. He was hurting; we could see it clearly. Ira asked him to phone Agnessa to come, but he declined.

A day before the performance Andrei declared that he wanted to return to Moscow. "Can't you wait for a day or two?" Ira must have implored him, but he stubbornly rejected all inducements. I called a taxi and went to the airport to see him off. The day was unusually hot. The rehearsals were tiresome, mostly because my migraines had returned with a vengeance. I wanted peace and quiet but to drive everyone away wasn't an option. I returned from the airport and was called into Gennady's room to join the party. It was a terrible decision. I should have gone back to my room to lie down. I didn't. It was a noisy party. People coming and going. Loud hellos, hugs and sloppy kisses. I was feeling hot and sweaty and I don't know who handed me a glass of wine. I took a sip, the glass slipped out of my hand and I collapsed.

Ira tells me that Andrei blames himself for the accident. He shouldn't. I have tried many times to reassure him that he should blame my excessive drinking instead. I was overworked and run down. "I know, I know," he tells me and smiles, and from the way he turns his head away, I sense that it won't be easy for him to find peace. I have my Father Nikolai, to whom I can confess and free myself. Andrei doesn't have anyone. He doesn't trust his mother anymore and it seems Agnessa too has been left behind.

However, it doesn't mean that we have lost each other completely. Moments of utter beauty do arrive unexpectedly, and because they come unannounced, an expectation, like a luminous cloud, lives in me. For instance, it's midnight and Andrei, to keep me company, has come to sit with me. Not to talk but just to share the blissful quietude.

"Tell me what's it like in heaven?" He suddenly asks

"What do you mean?"

"I mean on the other side. Did you really get to see Him?"

The brief chuckle with which I start my answer amuses him. He waits and then scared that the chuckle might be followed by a prolonged silence, repeats the question.

Unable to find the right words to satisfy him, I start to tell him about my dreams. He listens carefully and although I feel he thinks I am evading the question, the way he holds my hand in both his hands convinces me that he is willing to accept my stories. My story about Frau Ruber is utterly believable, and so is the story about Adrian Leverkuhn. However, I don't tell him that I did once meet Bach up there playing *Sarabande* on a French viola da gamba. I didn't tell him because it felt too fanciful. He wouldn't have believed me.

In the early hours of the following morning I suddenly hear a melodic line hum its way inside my mind. I open my eyes and see Ira standing in the door, dressed in a white gown, her right arm raised and behind her a trail of sunlight.

*

The cello concerto is finished. I am disappointed that it has turned out to be so melancholic. I wanted to write something as rapturous as Bach's *Gloria*, but it hasn't happened. I hope it does happen, and happens before I die.

A letter from a musicologist arrived two days ago. She plays cello and is writing a scholarly piece on my *Faust Cantata*. She wants to know if I can describe the moment or the circumstances in which I began to work on the piece.

I don't know what to say. It happened because it had to. Who cares how and when? Perhaps I should send her the pages I have scribbled the last few weeks. She may find in them the answer she is looking for. I know she will, because she is too anxious to find one.

She has spelt her name Saray, which Father Nikolai explains to me is the same as Sarah. "A very nice Biblical name," he says and tells me about the ninety-year old wife of Abraham, the mother of nations.

"How very mysterious," I say to myself, and open her letter again to have a look at her handwriting and notice that the letter is typed.

"Doesn't matter," I tell myself and as I begin to put the letter back in the envelope I notice the handwritten address. I touch the black letters. My fingers feel their shape and a melody begins to take form in my mind. It is a variation of the melody I heard when I saw Ira standing near the door in the early hours of that sunlit morning. She sings, but strangely the voice is that of a young contralto. It's Bach again.

Glossary of names

Pablo (Pau) Casals (1876-1973): Catalan cellist and conductor.

J. S. Bach (1685-1750): German composer and musician of the Baroque period.

Walter Benjamin (1892-1940): German-Jewish philosopher and literary critic.

Anna Dostoevskaya (1846-1918): The second wife of Fyodor Dostoevsky. She wrote two memoirs about her husband.

Fyodor Dostoevsky (1821-1881): Russian novelist, essayist and journalist. Holbein's *The Body of the Dead Christ in the Tomb* appears in his novel, *The Idiot*.

Hans Holbein, the younger (1497-1543): German artist and printmaker.

Georges Braque (1882-1963): French painter, printmaker and sculptor. He and Pablo Picasso (1881-1973) were friends and collaborated in developing cubism.

Henri Laurens (1885-1954): French cubist sculptor and illustrator.

Lev Tolstoy (1828-1910): Russian novelist, essayist and philosopher.

Atsuko Tanaka (1932-2005); Japanese painter, sculptor and performance artist. Member of the Gutai Group.

Merce Cunnignham (1919-2009): American dancer and choreographer.

Martin Heidegger (1889-1976): German philosopher.

Paul Celan (1920-1970): Jewish-Romanian poet and translator who wrote in German.

Alfred Schnittke (1934-1998): Soviet Russian-Jewish-German composer. He finished his *Faust Cantata* in 1983.

References

Benjamin, W. *Reflections: Essays, Aphorisms, Autobiographical Writing* (translated by Edmund Jephcott). New York: Schocken Books, 1986.

Brodersen, M. *Walter Benjamin: A Biography* (translated by Malcolm R. Green and Ingrida Ligers). London: Verso, 1996.

Casals, P. *Joys and Sorrows: His Own Story as Told to Albert E. Kahn*. London: Eeel Pie Publishing, 1981.

Cunningham, M., Lesschaeve, J. *The Dancer and the Dance: Merce Cunningham in conversation with Jacqueline Lesschaeve*. New York: Marion Boyars, 1985.

Danchev, A. *Georges Braque: A Life*. New York: Arcade Publishing, 2005.

Laurens, H. *Bronzes, Collages, Drawings, Prints: Catalogue of Exhibition*. London: Arts Council of Great Britain, 1980.

Dostoevskaya, A. G. *Vospominaniya*. Moskva: Khudozhestvennaya Literatura, 1968.

Grossman, L. P. *Dostoevsky*. Moskva: Moladaya Gvardiya, 1962.

Heidegger, M. *Being and Time* (translated by John Macquarie and Edward Robinson). New York: Harper One, 1962.

Ivashkin, A. *Alfred Schnittke*. London: Phaidon Press, 1996.

Kirk, H. L. *Pablo Casals a biography*. New York: Holt, Rinehart and Winston, 1974.

Okabe, A. *Atsuko Tanaka: Another Gutai* (Documentary Film). Tokyo: Ufer Art Documentary, 1998.

Shulgin, D. I. *Gody Neizvestnosti Alfreda Schnitke*. Moskva: Delovaya Liga, 1993.

Storer, R. *Paddy Bedford*. Sydney: Museum of Contemporary Art, 2007.

Taussig, M. *Walter Benjamin's Grave*. Chicago: University of Chicago Press, 1992.

Wilson, A. N. *Tolstoy*. London: Penguin Books, 1988.

Wolff, C. *Johann Sebastian Bach: The Learned Musician*. New York: W. W. Norton & Company, 2000.

Acknowledgements

I gratefully acknowledge the editors of *Conversation* (No. 2, 2005) for publishing an earlier version of 'Heidegger's Hammer', and of *Etchings* (No. 9, 2010) for publishing 'Bach (Pau) in Love'.

I am grateful to Arts ACT, Canberra, for providing a grant to assist the editing and printing of the book. I thank many friends who read one or more stories and helped me with their comments. They include: Stephanie Anderson, Roland Bleiker, Alex Danchev, Diana Giese, John Hughes, Gail Jones, Lois McRae, and Lycia Trouton. Maggie Cullen was gracious in translating a news report from a French newspaper. Mayke Kranenberg helped me with her knowledge of working with the Gija people at the Warmun Art Centre. I also thank Francesca Cubillo, for explaining me the production of blue colour in Aboriginal paintings. Many thanks go to Ed Wright for editing the manuscript. His comments were immensely valuable.

Dedications

'Bach (Pau) in Love' : To David Pereira; 'Walter Benjamin's Pipe': To John Docker; 'Anna and Fyodor in Basel': To John Hughes; 'The Electric Dress': To Lycia Trouton; 'Dance is Like Water': To David Musgrave; 'The Dreams of Johann Ulrich Voss': To Nick Jose; '*Faust Cantata*: Unreliable Notes for an Autobiography': To Caroline Stacey.